Praise for *One Arm Shorter*

"Gigi is the kind of writer who strives to bring light and joy into her readers' lives. *One Arm Shorter Than The Other* is a gorgeous, skillfully wrought, millennia-spanning feat of imagination, written with warmth and tenderness and great humour. I was enchanted by this novel, and uplifted. This kind of story is good for the soul."
  —Donal Ryan, four-time Irish Book Award winner

"I greatly admire Gigi Ganguly's vivid and beautiful writing, and I loved this novella."
  —Joseph O'Connor, award-winning novelist and Professor of Creative Writing

"An evocative mixture of psychological realism, magic realism, and the uncanny. From the Old Delhi setting to the ensemble cast of characters, all wounded by personal or family history, this is an extraordinary debut."
  —Jack Fennell, writer and anthologist

"A story that is both heartwarming and mind bending, *One Arm Shorter Than The Other* is a startlingly original work."
  —Wyn Lewis, Kid Ferrous Reviews, 5 Stars

"A wonderful mind-bending debut. The storyline set in historical India made me nostalgic for the street food!!"
  —Monika's Book Blog, 5 Stars

"Just amazing! From the setting in Delhi to the plot twists of each item and how they affect the owner after repair to the final story connecting them all, I highly recommend you read this."
  —Humaira Ahmad, Bookish Connections, 5 Stars

One Arm Shorter Than The Other

Gigi Ganguly

Detroit, Michigan

One Arm Shorter Than The Other

Edited by E.D.E. Bell

Cover Illustration by Haricha Abdaal

Interior Design by G.C. Bell and E.D.E. Bell

Published by Atthis Arts, LLC
Detroit, Michigan
atthisarts.com

ISBN 978-1-945009-77-8

Library of Congress Control Number: 2021947683

All characters in this story are fictional, for now.

Atthis Arts thanks the sensitivity reviewers, beta readers, and consultants who made this book flourish. In particular, our gratitude to Z. Ahmad and M. Kaur for your insights and care, and to Tony Eichenlaub for the perfect, thoughtful nudge when we were stuck.

For my parents

CHAPTERS

PROLOGUE

Noon-time sun is a different beast.

At dawn the sunlight is soft. It's gently prodding people to stop dreaming, to get out and start their day. By the time it's dusk, the light has lost its shine. It's drowsy, and is slowly lulling people to sleep as well, pushing them into their homes. But at midpoint, at 12 in the afternoon, the fiery watcher is wide awake, and there is a certain cruelty in its affection. It sees a young man, awkward in his steps, and lays a warm hand over his head, bearing down on him as he walks through the lanes of Chandni Chowk.

He seems to be new, unaware of his surroundings in the way a tourist usually is, and is following the path of a young woman in front of him. She is faster, used to the heat of noon, and is soon too far ahead of him.

She notices his absence and turns around, placing a hand over her brow, trying to block the sun from blinding her eyes. A minute later the man is next to her, sweltering, placing a white handkerchief against his forehead to wipe away the sweat. In the other hand he cradles a small bundle.

"It's too hot," he tells her.

"You're too slow," she tells him. And then smiles, reassuringly. "The shop isn't that far."

She is correct in her assessment, and only five minutes later they are at the doorstep of a two-tiered building. There is an attic at the top, but nobody lives there and no one even goes there for any purpose other than to look at the street below. It is the ground floor which is important, which stores broken objects and provides a place to work for the man who heals them. There are two windows on this floor, on either side of the main door, which allow the opportunity to look in. It's through these that the sunlight falls in, refracts, and lies down on the floor.

Inside, the man is much more comfortable. He visibly relaxes and sighs in relief, as he clutches the bundle to his chest and the woman says she's going to look around for her grandfather.

"He might be in the workshop," she tells the man, and moves towards a wooden door at the back of the room, leaving him in the company of shelves and cupboards that are at maximum occupancy. He looks at them—walks up to one glass-enclosed cupboard in particular which holds shelves of intricately carved wooden boxes, each pattern unique.

As he crouches down for a closer inspection, the woman comes back into the room with an old man trailing her. He addresses the young man, who straightens up and turns around, and the three of them laugh at something.

While the old man had been walking, his arms swinging by his side, it wasn't noticeable. But now that he has come to a stop in front of the young man and is talking to him about a broken vase, the discrepancy becomes quite evident, and the young man can't help but look and widen his eyes in surprise. Instantly, he is both apologetic and embarrassed about the staring, but the old man doesn't seem offended at all.

"It's human nature to be curious," he says. "And I don't mind. There aren't many in the world like me, with one arm shorter than the other."

PART I

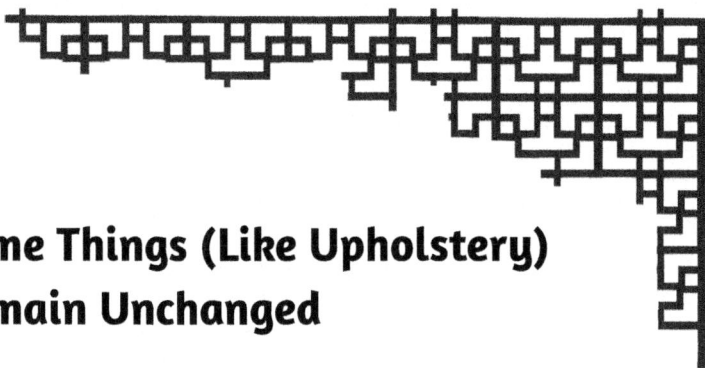

Some Things (Like Upholstery) Remain Unchanged

It's a slow oscillation towards death for his Eunice. There are days when there is a soft recognition in her eyes, when she is aware of her own predicament, and other days when a blank confusion clouds her vision. And she points to their son, James, the only one in the hospital room other than him, and asks, "Is that Horace? I thought he'd gone off to fight."

After a particularly good evening, during which she talks in whispered nostalgia about the time the three of them went to India Gate, the WWI memorial at the heart of Delhi, for some ice cream in the middle of the night, Maurice convinces himself that she might just be able to recover. The doctors are less optimistic, and tell him to be prepared for the worst. But he's not ready. He watches her sleep late into the night, refusing to leave just yet. He looks at her closed eyelids that are twitching with untamed movement and lips that are moving with unuttered words.

"Do you think she's dreaming of us?" he asks James.

"I don't know."

He not only sounds tired and defeated, but when Maurice turns to look him in the eye, he looks it too. "Is your leg okay?" he asks his son, who is standing lopsided, leaning on the left one. "We're in a hospital; we could get a check-up."

"I'm okay, Dad. It doesn't hurt . . . it's just something that happens when I'm . . . anxious. It's more of a psychological thing."

"Are you sure?" Maurice doesn't want anyone in his family to be in pain.

"I am. But I think we should go home and rest for a while," he adds. "You need some sleep, too. Come on, let's go home."

Maurice produces a sound akin to affirmation that turns into a gasp midway. He makes no move to stand up, but his son takes him by the shoulders and helps him up. Step by step they move towards the door and leave the room.

His Eunice dies a few hours later, still deep in her sleep.

He's in a new setup now, at their son's home in Civil Lines, north of where they used to live in Delhi. He understands the reasoning behind it: he can no longer live alone in the old, crumbling house in Chandni Chowk, the home he and Eunice had spent most of their lives in. But still, he can't help but feel even more alone in an alien environment, more like a guest than anything else. And yes, he is surrounded by his son and daughter-in-law, Helen, and his two grandchildren—Mary and Sebastian—but sometimes it all just makes things worse.

To see them young and happy, with their entire lives ahead of them, makes him crawl further into his web of nostalgia. And he finds himself, in waking dreams and night-time imaginations, thinking back on the times gone by, to a time when not only Eunice, but his brother, Horace, too, was alive.

Sometimes, at night, he sits alone in his room and goes through old family albums. He doesn't know if his dreams cause him to do this or the act of rifling through photographs lead him to his nostalgic wanderings. The one thing he is sure of, though, is that if he shares his thoughts with James and family they would term his actions "unhealthy" and tell him that "no good could come from dwelling on the past and forgetting to live in the present." He's heard those words before, from his father. Only, last time, after the war, Eunice was there to help him process his grief.

So when, at lunch and dinner, and any other time in between, his son looks at him with worried eyes, Maurice fears he'll see through his innermost thoughts and be disappointed with him. And he can't do anything but turn his face away, hide the truth before it gets laid out in the open.

He hopes this feeling passes, for then he'll find some peace. But until it does, he swims in his memories.

One day, while searching for more photos and letters, he comes across an old reel of film in a large, hitherto unopened suitcase of his. The reel is safe and secure, and has the year '1942' painted in his once-young handwriting on its case. He picks it up, blows the dust off its surface, and sets it aside on his bedside table. *There must be more in there,* he thinks, as he dives deeper into the suitcase, taking out two more reels. One is marked '1938' and another is labelled '1941'. He places them both next to the first one, and closes the suitcase.

Now, he works his mind to think where his projector might be.

"Grandpa Maurice?" a muffled voice comes from the other side of his bedroom door.

"Yes?"

"We heard you shuffling things in there. Do you want our help?"

"What do you mean by 'we'?"

"Seb is here, too."

"Hello, Grandpa," says the 11-year-old. He is a bit timid, apt to follow his 15-year-old sister everywhere. Even at Wisdom Public School, where they both study, he'll run to her if he sees her in the hallway—in between classes or during the lunch break.

"We can help you, if you want?" Mary tries again. "It doesn't sound like you're moving boxes now. Sounds heavier. And we thought we'd be able to . . ."

"Yes," Maurice answers. "Come on in. The door is open."

"So what are we looking for?" the girl wonders once both she and her brother are inside the room.

"A projector," he answers, as he sits on his bed, only then realising how his back has been straining with all the effort. "Like the ones in cinema halls. Have you seen one?" The kids nod their heads excitedly, and he watches as Mary and Seb take over and work as a team to find the missing machine.

"I think I might have found it," Seb says excitedly a while later. He opens a bundled-up blanket, coughing as the dust gets loose in the process, and looks at his grandfather. "Is this it?"

Maurice stands up, with Mary giving him a hand, and stands

over Seb and the open suitcase. "Oh yes," he says. "Thank you, Seb. Both of you, actually. Thank you so much."

"What should we do next?" Mary asks, looking at him eagerly. Her brother has the same expression on his face.

Maurice beams widely at them both. "Why," he says, "we must see if it works."

———◦———

It's Mary and Seb, again, who do the work for him, asking him at every turn if they are doing things the right way.

"Yes," he tells them. "You two are doing a good job. Just be careful, the reels can be quite delicate."

In the end, when everything is where it should be, and the '1942' reel is ready to roll, all three of them huddle together on the bed and try to sit still.

"What if it doesn't work?" Seb asks.

"Then we will get it repaired," Mary answers. "There's a place near where you used to live, Grandpa. We'll just take the projector there."

"When did you go there?" Maurice wonders.

"I found it when I accidentally broke Dad's camera. I would have gone into the shop then, but Dad said he knew another place and took me there."

"Oh?" Maurice asks. "What is the place called?"

"I can't remember; it was a very common name. But I have an idea about its location. I'm sure I'll find it when I go there."

"Hmm. Before we get ahead of ourselves, let's first see if

this works, shall we?" Maurice says, getting up from the bed with Seb's help and walking over to the machine in question. He switches it on, smiling, as he hears the gears jump into action.

"Mary, switch off the light, will you?" he says, and his granddaughter does just that, before moving back to the bed.

The film on the white wall livens up the room for a few seconds and he catches a glimpse of a young Eunice in a sparse and quiet Connaught Place—completely different from its current incarnation. And then the projector splutters and slows down, and dies pathetically. He looks back at his grandchildren, expecting them to look sad, but instead they seem even more excited.

"Does this mean we get to go out now?" Seb asks.

"Let's go find your parents," Maurice answers, "see what they have to say."

They head into the living room, to check with James and Helen if it's okay to travel to Old Delhi. But they seem so happy just at the announcement of an excursion that they don't ask for further details beyond what's in the suitcase that Mary and Seb are carrying.

Later, inside the taxi James has hailed for them, Seb sits in the front, and Mary and Maurice take up space at the back. The suitcase rests between them.

"When did you buy the projector?" Mary asks him a few minutes into their trip, as Seb (who is currently obsessed with a book about cars and trucks) indulges in a conversation about the best kind of wheels with the driver. "You never told us."

"A long time ago," Maurice answers. "Before even your

Dad was born. The year was 1936, when the British were still in control of the country . . ."

"Your father was one, wasn't he?" She interrupts him, eager to know more about her past. And Maurice is suddenly reminded of the time Seb was born, when Mary didn't quite understand why her mother was at the hospital. She had sought her grandfather's advice on the matter and, having been satisfied with his answers, had asked him one final question: "Where is your Mummy?"

She had passed away a long time ago, when Maurice himself was very young. But he couldn't tell her that. He couldn't tackle the subjects of birth and death in the same sitting, so, instead, he had told Mary about *where* her great-grandmother was from. Embellishing the details a little bit, he had told her that his mother was out hunting monsters. That she was most probably hiding in the southern part of the country, in a place called Kerala. "It's rumoured that she was born there," he had added in a whisper.

"Rumo?" she had asked quizzically.

"Sorry. What I meant to say was, 'People *say* that she was born in Kerala'. But no one knows for sure. She could be living under the sea, or high up in the mountains, or maybe," he had replied, lowering his voice, "she is here in Delhi, in disguise . . . wearing a costume, protecting us from monsters of all kinds."

"Really, Grandpa?" she had asked. And he had nodded most solemnly, trying not to smile at the wide-eyed look on her face.

She has the same expression now, waiting on Maurice to speak about his father. There is a hint of worry, too, for he has taken a bit too long to answer her question.

He clears his throat as he opens his mouth once more. "My

father . . ." he says, reminiscing. "Yes, he was born and brought up in England. But he came here when he was in his early 20s, broke his leg during a game of cricket, met my mother—who was a doctor—at the hospital, and stayed on."

"He was a complicated man," he continues. "It almost felt like he was stuck between two places, and he couldn't quite figure out where he belonged. This constant turmoil inside him made him a difficult man, as well—stubborn in what he wanted, cold when confronted with emotions."

"You know," Maurice says, voice growing softer, "when my mother died, he was just as cold and stoic. I was younger than even Seb when she passed away. I was confused and scared, but my father refused to talk about her after she passed. All I remember is she got very ill very fast, and in a few months she was dead."

There is a stillness in the car, before Mary asks, "What was she like?"

"I don't have many memories of her," Maurice answers, "but the ones I have are so strong that I'm often swept away. Sometimes I'll come across a flowery scent that will remind me of her. Or there will be thunder and lightning in the sky and it will take me back to the time we spent at her parents' house."

Mary falls silent as she considers the answer while Seb turns around to look at his grandfather. Tentatively, as if he's been wondering about this question for some time, he asks, "Wasn't your father sad when she died?"

"He most definitely was. He loved her very much. But he never showed that side to us. As I told you before—he was a complicated man. He had good sides and bad. He gave us a lot of fiscal freedom. He allowed us to follow our dreams, no matter how outlandish they sounded. He was a businessman—he was the one who founded the textile company your Dad heads now—and he had a lot of money to spare. And so, whenever we asked him for money, he always gave us the amount without any question."

"What do you mean by 'we'?" Seb asks.

"My brother Horace and I. James never got to meet him. He died before that could . . ."

Mary seems saddened by the fact that a part of her history had been kept away from her. "I didn't know you had a brother," she says.

But then she straightens up and looks at him with renewed interest. "What happened in 1936? What were you going to say?"

"That was the year Horace and I went up to our father and asked if we could get some money to open our own cinema hall."

"What?" Seb asks, turning his head once more. "Why didn't anyone tell us about this?"

Because those were the happiest and also the saddest years of my life, Maurice thinks.

"Because it was all such a long time ago," he says, staring outside into the crowded streets. He sees the people, of course. Some of them are in a hurry and have a constant frown on their face as they navigate the slow-walkers, those who have all the time in the world. He sees, too, the buildings—the ones he's grown up with and the ones that have cropped up post-Independence, in the 1950s, and he suddenly feels the weight of all his years, piling upon him with eight decades of fear, happiness, and despair.

He drives a hand through his snow-white hair, to push some of those feelings away.

"What was it called?" Mary asks him then. "The movie hall?"

"Horace and Maurice's Cinema Palace," he says, chuckling, looking back at her. "We were quite proud of the name."

The children laugh, too, as does the driver.

"That sounds very dramatic," Mary says.

"And it was; with red and gold seats inside the halls and a Roman palace-like facade outside. We bought the screen, and even this projector here, from Germany. In those days, that was the place where all the advancements in movie-making were being made. Horace knew that, and insisted that we source everything from there. He was practically obsessed with German cinema, too, at that time."

"Where was it, your cinema palace?" Seb asks.

"In Connaught Place. I operated it for a few years before selling it in the 40s. I think the new owners renamed it Royale Palace."

"Oh," Mary says. "I've been there! The seats inside are still red and gold."

"Are they now? That's good. I've never found the desire to go back." He had tried to have a look inside, in the 60s, but all he'd thought about was Horace, and how much he'd have loved to see his cinema still functioning, filled up with people. And so he had left the hall without even watching the film he had bought a ticket for.

But he doesn't tell his grandchildren that part. He looks out the window again, into his old neighbourhood, as the taxi leans to the left and slows to a halt next to the pavement.

"We're here," the driver says. "You'll have to walk a bit to the market. I can't go any farther; I'll get stuck in traffic. A rickshaw would have fared better on these roads, but . . ."

"I know, young man," Maurice answers, handing him the fare. "I used to live here."

When they get out, Seb and Mary carry the suitcase between them as they stride ahead of Maurice. From time to time, they stop, rest their hands and check to see if their grandfather is still following them.

The street they are walking on seems familiar, and he wonders if he's ever wandered these parts with either Horace or Eunice. He must have, he thinks.

When he was young, all he ever did was travel with his camera to different parts of Delhi. (A lot of times Horace and Eunice tagged along.) He spent some time in Hauz Khas, in the south, before it became the popular marketplace it is now, and took pictures of the lake and the historical ruins on site. He went to the Red Fort, where every year, on Independence Day, the Prime Minister delivers his or her speech. He travelled to the Lodhi Gardens, the vast expanse of green frequented by peacocks and other birds; and to the Qutub Minar, the 12th century tower of bricks that stands tall to this day. He knows he visited these places, these historical sites, because he's found pictures to support his claim.

There are several more boxes and suitcases, filled with more such photos, lying in James' garage, which he hasn't even touched yet. It's not disinterest on his part, but a side-effect of his age. At 80, he is no longer the man who could walk for hours out in the sun, with his camera swung over his shoulders, eagerly hoping for the light to hit just right.

It's been a while they've been walking, and he's glad that, at least, it's not the height of summer. It's only a few days into January, when the sun, though bright, isn't as harsh.

"Where did you say this shop was?" he asks Mary.

"I think we are quite close," his granddaughter answers. "If I remember correctly, it should be . . . there, it's only a few feet away. Can you see it? The board says 'Repair Services'."

He stops a metre away, looks at the building from the bottom to the top; noticing the windows, the walls, and the attic up above. It's there that his eyes linger and stop. The window is closed shut, but the curtains are open, and for a moment it reminds him of when he was 10 years old, and a 4-year-old Horace would look out the second-floor of their childhood home, make use of the vantage point, to wave at him on the days he would go to school. *He couldn't wait to become a schoolboy himself,* Maurice thinks. *He was always so eager about new adventures.*

"Grandpa?" Seb's voice stirs him from the memory.

"Yes?"

"Aren't you coming in? Mary is already inside and we've placed the suitcase there."

"Oh, of course," he says, moving towards the teak door. He feels someone's eyes on him, from the masses on the road. But when he turns around, he can't see anyone paying close attention to him.

"Grandpa?"

"Coming," he says, opening the door. "I'm not as young as you."

Inside, Maurice thinks he has travelled back in time (and place). His nose registers the scent of age and memories as his eyes settle on the objects around him. On shelves and inside cupboards, there are telephones and typewriters, and toasters and television sets. And some gadgets that he has no idea what they could be used for. There's a grandfather clock as well, near a door at the back.

His grandchildren walk up to the gadgets in awe, talking amongst themselves, wondering what the more unusual-looking ones could be. There's one, Maurice notices, that looks like a teapot but is behaving like a Jack-in-the-box, opening its lid in intervals of a few seconds and pouring out some water, which is being drained into the bottom of the teapot, only for the process to repeat again.

"Can I buy that, Grandpa?" Seb asks, giggling. He knows what the answer will be, but is compelled to ask nevertheless.

"I don't think so, Seb," Maurice replies.

On his right, where there's a counter, he can see Mary already in conversation with a young woman in her 20s, who's in a pink, embroidered salwar kameez, with a dark pink dupatta. Her hair is as long as Mary's, and is also tied up in a simple ponytail.

"I was just telling . . ." Mary begins uncertainly.

"Jaya," the young woman supplements.

"I was just telling Jaya that you built the Royale Palace," Mary continues, as he holds Seb's hand and shuffles over to stand next to her, his granddaughter who is beaming at him, so proud of his accomplishments. "And that this very projector," she points at the suitcase next to her feet, "was used inside the cinema hall. Isn't that right, Grandpa?"

Maurice smiles. "Yes, initially, we used this projector. But later on we realised this was too small, so we ordered a bigger one from Bombay. I forget what it was called, but it was being used everywhere in those days."

"It must have been very exciting," Jaya says, smiling. "To establish something from scratch."

"It was. We spent months finding the right colour, the right material for everything. I think we bought some things from Chandni Chowk itself."

A door opens, the one next to the grandfather clock, and a man who looks to be the same age as him saunters into the room. He's in a simple pair of kurta and pajama. And his face is clean-shaven and friendly, where Maurice's own is marked by an overgrown beard that has taken over most of his neck.

"Hello," the man gently greets, waving a hand at them.

"This is my Dadaji," Jaya introduces him.

"That means 'grandfather' in Hindi," Mary whispers to Seb.

"I know." Seb replies softly. He'd only recently stopped calling their father 'Dada', when he'd realised most of his class-mates thought he'd been talking about his grandpa.

". . . and he will repair your projector," Jaya finishes speaking.

The man in question finally reaches the counter and stands behind it, next to Jaya. "A projector?" His eyebrows lift up. "Why, I've not repaired one since the 50s. Where did you find this?" He directs this question to all three.

"I bought this from Germany in 1936," Maurice answers.

"My brother was the one who found it in a catalogue and ordered it." He chortles as he remembers. "I had no say in the matter."

Dadaji, Jaya, and the kids chuckle.

"I remember the first time I saw a film in the theatre," Dadaji says. "I can't recall the exact name . . . Maybe Ho-rse . . . Place? I'm not sure . . ."

Mary and Seb let out a gasp, and Maurice himself sounds incredulous. "Do you mean Horace and Maurice's Cinema Palace? That's the one my brother and I built."

"Is that right?" Dadaji grins. "How fascinating. Which one are you?"

"I'm Maurice. My brother . . . he was Horace. He passed away a long time ago." He lets out a cough in discomfort, and Jaya, noticing it, herds the children and takes them for a little walk around the shop. As they walk away, Seb asks her about the shelves and why they are so full. And Jaya responds saying that sometimes people return things because they don't like them anymore, sometimes Dadaji builds odd objects of his own, and some other times people just don't return for their belongings.

"He died during the war, the second one," Maurice adds when the children are out of earshot. "He was so very young."

"And you've suffered a recent loss as well," Dadaji notes. He says it very gently.

"Eunice. My wife," is all he says, before slightly changing the direction of the conversation by patting the suitcase near his feet. "The reels that go with this projector . . . they are all about Horace and Eunice."

"I see," Dadaji says, his eyes crinkling in thought. "Well, let me have a look then," he says, as he comes out of the counter and kneels down near the suitcase.

Maurice is a bit surprised at the ease with which he does it, but he doesn't remark on it. The repairman is obviously more fit than him, and he doesn't want to call attention to that fact.

"This is magnificent," Dadaji says, having opened the suitcase. He lightly touches the projector, using both his hands to skim over the contents. It is then that Maurice notices his arms—how the left one is several inches shorter than the right one.

"When was the last time you used this?" Dadaji asks, still looking down.

"Around the time James was born—my son—the kids' father." He is still preoccupied with the other man's left arm, and feels the need to share more. "James . . . he was a very naughty child, you know. Very adventurous. A few months after we bought him a motorcycle for his 18th birthday, he crashed it and seriously injured himself. They had to amputate his left leg in the end."

"Oh," Dadaji says, as he stands up. "Did everything . . ."

"He's fine now. More than fine. As he grew older, the wild edge left him and he became more mature, more responsible. Eunice and I were quite relieved with that," he laughs.

Dadaji politely smiles at him.

"So what do you think about the projector?" Maurice asks. "Do you need more time to go through it, figure things out?"

"Oh no. There's no need for that. Leave it with me for an hour, and I'll fix it. I guarantee it."

"What will we do till then?" Seb's voice comes from the door of the workshop. Jaya and Mary are standing behind him.

Maurice doesn't have a clear plan in mind, but Mary comes to the rescue and says, quite simply, "Should we go eat?"

———o———

The restaurant is largely unchanged since the last time he visited the place, with Eunice in the 70s. The chairs look just as weary, the menu card just as torn, although he's not sure if the walls were that yellow all those years ago. He's glad though, that the smell and taste of the food hasn't changed one bit. The spices, the herbs, the gravy are just as delicious as they were then.

When they return to the shop, eyes heavy with sleep from having eaten so much—kebabs, naan, dal makhani, and tandoori chicken— they think they are hallucinating when Dadaji switches on the projector. Their vision seems to be moving along with the visuals on the thin white cloth they are using as a screen. Why, Maurice half-wonders, it almost feels like they are in the film itself.

A while later, all three rub their eyes and widen their mouths in yawns; as they thank Dadaji and Jaya for their service, as Maurice pays them 400 rupees, which he thinks is a decent amount, and as they leave the place with the projector in tow. They walk a little distance, before a taxi driver accosts them and they haggle their way inside it. Half an hour later, they are back at home and in their beds for a nap.

When they wake up, sometime around 4 in the evening, all three of them feel woozy, and Maurice wonders if their food had been drugged.

"No," his son chortles when he suggests that. "It's just that you all had a lot of rich food, out in the sun. It made you a bit sleepy. The ride back home must have exacerbated that."

They all have tea, even the kids, who usually detest the beverage and ask for a fizzier one. It is a compromise that must be made, since they are in need of wakefulness. Their grandfather has promised them the opportunity to watch at least one video reel when they are all free. It incentivises them to quickly complete their homework, eat their dinner and brush their teeth, before heading into Maurice's room for their own little film festival.

James doesn't encroach on this time; he realises it's special and meant only for his children and his father. But he does tell them to be in bed by 11 pm. "No later than that."

All three of them nod at him in impatience, waiting for him to leave so they can close the door. And James chuckles at their behaviour, happy despite their annoyance at him. He's been carrying his camera with him all this while, letting the strap hang from his shoulders. And now he brings it in front of his face, tells them to smile—Seb chooses to stick out his tongue—and clicks a picture for posterity.

———◦———

When at last the room is dark and the projector is set—the curtains having been drawn to the full extent so as to not let the moonlight into the room—Seb fits the '1942' reel in place and returns to sit with his sister and grandfather. He is just in time to see the visuals light up the wall.

"Wow," he lets out in the same breath as Maurice gasps and Mary opens her mouth in silent amazement.

There, right there, on the white background is a very young Eunice, dark-haired and smooth-skinned, beaming at the camera. It feels very real, as if they are standing right in front of her. They can hear her, too—the soft, gentle curls of laughter. But more than that, they can feel her presence, and the crisp scent of the morning. And even though they *know* the film is in black and white, they can see the colour of her clothes, the off-white tone of the Connaught Place buildings behind her, and the light blue of the sky above. The scene changes in an instant, and they are in a room. There is a baby in the cot, a sleeping one.

"That's James," Maurice tells Mary and Seb. His voice echoes from all directions, inside his current bedroom and the one his son inhabited when he was a year old. "I joined two reels together for this one. I think I filmed them within a week of each other."

Again, their senses are heightened. They can see, smell, hear, and feel everything at once. As if they are right there, with baby James. Mary takes it a step further and tries to touch the cot her father lies in. She immediately jumps back while doing so, when her fingers encounter the actual bars of the crib.

At the exact same moment, there is a click signalling the end and the reel stops playing. Mary, whose arm is still in the position of recoil, looks back at Maurice and Seb who are just as shocked as her.

"What just happened?" she asks.

"Are all projectors like that?"Seb enquires.

"No," Maurice says. "I have never . . . never seen anything like this."

"Where were you?" his granddaughter asks.

"What do you mean? I was right here on the bed."

"No. Why weren't you there?" She points at the wall.

"I was behind the camera, of course."

"Do you still have it?" Seb asks.

"No. I . . . broke it by accident."

There are a few seconds of quiet between them, before Mary asks, "Do you think we should check the other reels too?"

"Yes," Maurice says. "Definitely."

They watch a youthful Horace running around in a park in the year 1938. His expression is animated and he's making faces at them. They watch a shy Eunice, too, having recently married Maurice in 1941, looking at the camera and blushing. Throughout it all, Mary, Seb, and their grandfather feel as if they are right there, and any wrong movement on their part will make them bump into their dead relatives. No one tries what Mary had earlier attempted. It seems like crossing a barrier of sorts, to actually touch them.

When it is over, when they have seen the visuals a second time over again, all three of them break into varying degrees of disbelief, excitement, and relief. And they decide right then and there that they will inform James and Helen in the morning.

"But nobody else," Mary adds. "This should be a family secret; meant only for us. You can't tell anyone at school, okay Seb? Not even that nice librarian who lets you borrow extra books."

Her brother makes the action of zipping his lips, and nods his head.

"First thing tomorrow," Maurice tells the children as they get up from the bed to leave, "we'll show your parents what we have experienced."

He doesn't think he'll be able to rest, what with all that has happened in the past one hour. However, as his head gently hits the pillows, his eyes instantly close and he falls into a dreamless sleep. When he wakes up the next day, his eyes open to the projector, standing in the middle of the room with an unaffected air. Maurice sits up with a groan, sends prayers to the repairman who worked magic on his old machine, and moves out of his room to prepare his son for what he's about to witness.

———————◦———————

"Is that real? What is . . . ?" James says softly, after he's watched all three videos. His pupils are wide when the light is switched on in the room, more out of fear than anything else. Helen, next to him, is still too shocked to ask a question.

"Does that mean?" his son starts again. "What does that mean?"

"Just that," Maurice says, "we can actually be with Eunice and Horace, and even you, in that moment with them. And all of it is real. Your mind isn't playing tricks on you, if that's what you're wondering."

Helen bursts out with exclamations right then, having recovered her thoughts. "This is so exciting," she says, proceeding to hug her children. But her husband only frowns as he drags his gaze from the projector to his grinning father. There is a questioning concern in his eyes and again Maurice turns away from him, choosing instead to join his daughter-in-law and grandchildren in their celebration.

It becomes a ritual of sorts, from that day on, with Mary and Seb moving to Maurice's room in the night to watch the films. They talk about things, too, but only at the end of the viewing and only if one of them has noticed something interesting in the visuals. But soon enough, an unsettlement creeps in. The children get bored of watching the same thing over and over again, and their grandfather gets frustrated with how little of his memories he can experience like this. He wants more such films, more such moments.

"Do we *have* to watch a film today?" It's Seb who says that. Perhaps he's less afraid of hurting Maurice's feelings.

"What should we do then?"

"We can talk," Mary replies. "You never told us why you sold your movie hall. We can watch something after you tell us the reason, if you want."

"Okay," he tells them, deciding that he'll tell them the entirety of what happened to Horace, that there was no point in keeping things hidden from his grandchildren.

"What was it that I told you last?" he asks.

"That your movie hall was renamed 'Royale Palace'," Mary helps.

"Oh, yes. But let me tell you what happened before that. The first few years were wonderful. The era of silent films was done with, and movies had the feature of sound added to them. Audiences all over the world were enraptured; they had never seen something like that before. Everywhere on Earth, cinema was changing. It seemed poised to rule this planet, no one could stop it. Even when trouble started brewing in 1939, movie-making did not stop. As people began to die in thousands, as the world dived headfirst into its second war, the hope that films represented didn't diminish. It only grew."

"Our movie hall would have grown too," Maurice continues, "if it weren't for our father's desire to see one of his sons fight for his motherland, for England. Already soldiers here were heading to Europe to fight the Nazis, and Father wanted us as a family to do our part for the cause. He let us decide who was to go, not caring how difficult it was to choose who was to be sent off to die in a foreign place."

He pauses, staring at the '1941' reel-case. "I had just met your grandmother and I already knew I was going to marry her. And Horace, well, he had dreams of becoming a filmmaker. He wanted to go to Bombay and learn the craft."

"There was no way," he adds, "I could ask him to sacrifice himself for me and there was no way he would ask the same of me. But I was older than him, and there was a need in me to protect him. Horace, on the other hand, always and I mean always, worried about me. But where I took my time to make a decision, my brother was quick and determined. And that was why he went directly to our father and told him he would be the one to join the war."

"Why did he do that?" Seb asks.

"He joked; said he knew I was too weak to go into battle. But he also told me he wanted me to have a family, to stay on in Delhi and support Father and his company. I was more suited to a stable life like that; he was the one who took risks. And that was true . . . but I also got the feeling his readiness to go to Europe, to go to Germany, stemmed from his desire to visit the land of his cinematic dreams."

"And then what happened?" Mary asks.

"He died. He went to Germany, where the closest he ever came to filmmaking was a bullet-ridden movie hall in a small town. Right after that, he was marched into the Battle of Monte Cassino in Italy where, on March 24, 1944, he got shot by an Axis soldier and died."

"Oh," says Seb.

"I'm so sorry, Grandpa," adds Mary.

He nods at them as he continues. "The day I received the news, I made some enquiries and sold Horace and Maurice's Cinema Palace to the first bidder. I wasn't in the right frame of mind, and in my anger I even destroyed the camera that produced these reels. Eunice stopped me from attacking the projector and the videos, hiding them away in these suitcases. And after a month or two, I joined Father's company. I was extremely upset with him, of course. But I remembered what my brother had wanted and I didn't want to cause him any worry, even though he was no longer around."

Maurice speaks no more, feeling his eyes grow heavy with

tears. He doesn't want to look at the kids; he doesn't think he'll be comfortable to see their downturned faces. So he stares ahead at the projector, till the emotional storm inside him calms again. There is no other sound in the room, not until a few minutes later when James knocks on the door and the hypnotic element is broken.

"It's already 11," he tells his children. "You two need to go to sleep."

He is sure to have noticed the atmosphere in the bedroom, but he doesn't say anything until his kids have returned to their beds.

"Are you alright?" James asks softly, keeping his distance from the projector.

"I'm fine. Thank you," Maurice answers, looking up at him.

His son gives him half a grin. "Mary told me we're not going to share this . . . with anyone? Is that right?"

"Yes."

"So you're going to keep this with you? Watch the reels over and over again? Are you sure that's a good idea?"

"What else is there to do?"

"I thought you were enjoying spending time with your grandkids; talking to them about your life."

"I was. I am."

"Isn't that enough?" James asks. And this time Maurice can't look anywhere, as worry fills his son's eyes. In this light, with the shadows that are being cast on his face, James looks just like Horace.

A flicker of a memory lights up his mind then and he remembers a terrible monsoon storm at his maternal grandparents' house in Kerala, where the thunder was so loud that Horace and he were both shaking in fear under their blanket. It's clear as day to Maurice, the look of worry on his little brother's face—that was only soothed when their mother came into the room, singing them a song in her native Malayalam. Later, she clasped their hands, took them to the kitchen and gave them each a glass of warm milk. She told them not to worry, that the sound outside was of monsters crying out because they didn't like being wet in the rain.

"What if," Horace had asked, voice wavering, "they come into the house?"

"I'll never let that happen," their mother had replied, softly running a hand through his hair. "I'll protect you both," she had said, enveloping her sons in a hug.

"Are you alright?" James asks once more, as Maurice shivers from the memory and sees shades of Horace's concern etched into his son's face.

Horace had been the strong one, who'd always looked out for him; who always, in all matters, only ever wanted the best for his big brother.

"Actually, James?" Maurice says, in a bit of a trance still. "I need your help with something."

"Of course," his son says, coming over to sit beside him.

"Can you pack the projector back inside the suitcase, please?" he asks.

James beams and nods his head. But as he gets up, Maurice calls out to him again.

"I have one more request."

"Sure. What is it?" James stands still in front of him.

"Do you think . . . Would it be possible to go on a trip?"

His son is a bit apprehensive. "Where do you want to go?" he still asks.

"Veettileke," Maurice answers. *Home.*

"Kerala," he clarifies. "I'd like to take the kids."

Be Careful With The TV Settings

"I don't know how to tell you, Paritosh, but . . ."

"I didn't get the part?"

"I tried to get you a smaller role, but they declined that, too."

"I see."

"You still have that light bulb company ad."

"Please don't remind me."

"It won't be that bad, Paritosh."

"Oh, sorry. It'll be *wonderful*. Is that better?"

"I didn't mean it th . . ."

"Goodbye," he says, before banging the receiver in place.

He lets out a sound that's between a groan and a growl. And then he gets up from his seat on the sofa, even though the depression in the cushion makes it difficult for him to perform such an action. For a second he loses his balance, but then he settles down on his feet and makes his daily pilgrimage to the TV set to switch it on from the plug point.

It is a slightly inconvenient action, since the TV is fitted inside an old teak cabinet (a gift from his in-laws) which is stuffed with crystal dolphins, ceramic vases, and Ganeshas and Durgas of varying sizes—and the plug itself can be accessed only through a little gap in the wooden shelves. He's always afraid of knocking over a vase, or damaging one of the figurines.

He could, he knows, keep the TV switched on from the plug point, but he doesn't want to spend any extra money the standby appliance could incur. So he manoeuvres his hand in between the wood, blindly flips down the switch, and then carefully extracts his limb from the cabinet.

Once he does that, he saunters back to his perch and settles in comfortably. From where he sits, on one of the two sofa chairs on the opposite side of the TV cabinet, he has a clear view of the entire room. On his right is the three-seater sofa, the main door of the flat just beyond that. And on his left is the open space that leads to the dining area and the other rooms beyond.

It isn't a huge place—their compact flat in Malviya Nagar— but since his wife and daughters are not home at the moment, even a small home such as theirs seems vast and empty. The need to watch some TV, to hear a voice that's not his own, is a means for him to fill this emptiness.

He feels the weight of the remote as he considers this, as he presses down on the power button and the blank screen crackles to life. Immediately he lets out an "Ugh" when the face of a young actor fills up his television. He has no talent, this supposed "superstar", everyone knows that. But his parents and grandparents have all been actors and directors before, so no one dares say that to his face.

He stays with that channel for a while, noticing how the man on screen can't even emote or properly say his dialogues. When he is angry, he shouts; when he is drunk, he exaggerates slurring his speech. *Horrible, just plain horrible,* he muses. And yet, the star-kid is still getting films, while Paritosh, a much superior actor, is sitting inside his house on a Monday morning with nothing to do but watch television.

He knows he does this a lot—complain about the acting capabilities of other actors and actresses. His daughters, Indrani and Nandini, both say he often ruins films by talking over the dialogues to list out the many on-screen faults. He gets their point of view, he really does. But it's very tough for him to stay quiet when he sees such horrendous artistry.

Paritosh himself was never like that. Since he was a child, people praised him for his performances in school plays, college theatre productions, and even silver-screen films. He had . . . no, he *has* a natural ability to inhabit any character's shoes. He can cry at the drop of a hat, appear happy and cheerful one second, and disappointed and disheartened the next.

In his very first film, when he was only 21, he played a background character with just one line. Yet, he caught Lalit's eye and became a client of his. Through the contacts of his agent, he progressed from the background to the foreground, from a driver to the hero's best friend, and then the hero himself. It took him close to five years to accomplish that.

But then, as the world entered another decade and the 80s became all about disco, Paritosh found himself sidelined. He was only 40, in 1988, when he got his first role as a "father".

To say he was miffed would be an understatement. But still, he accepted the role, and even won a nomination at one of the many acting awards in existence. It was a travesty, to say the least, but what added to his annoyance was that he never got any "superstar" treatment. He came very close to it in the late 1970s, when he had a few leading roles, but it brushed past him, never to return. And before he could have any say in his own life, he was deemed too old to be the lead anymore.

Lalit came up with a solution. "Don't kill me for saying this," he said over coffee at the Leopold Café in Bombay, sometime in 1991. "Please think it over, what I'm about to say, and then make a decision."

Paritosh was ready with an angry retort, suspicious that he'll have to accept a humiliating solution, when Lalit added a "Don't shout at me, either" to his earlier request.

Even though Paritosh nodded his head in compliance, with a grumpy sigh to accompany his action, Lalit pushed his coffee out of Paritosh's reach before uttering, "It might be a good idea to move back to Delhi . . ."

"I'm not . . ."

". . . for a while, at least."

"But there are no acting jobs there, other than theatre. And there's no money in that!"

"That's why you'll also work on a serial. It's called '*Dilli ki Rooh*'—which means 'The Soul of Delhi' in Urdu."

"I know what 'rooh' means," Paritosh interrupts, but Lalit ignores him.

"There's a perfect role for you in it."

"I'm not going to play the father."

"Of course not. You will be the protagonist's uncle. A rich bachelor who acts as the bad guy sometimes."

"A TV villain?" Paritosh sounds sceptical.

"I thought you'd always wanted to try an evil role?"

"Yes, but television is so . . . I don't know. It's just that people usually step up from TV shows to films. No one goes the other way around. It's . . . It's embarrassing. What will people think of me? That I can't find work anywhere and have to . . ."

"Believe me," Lalit said, putting a stop to his monologue. "It's the best choice for you right now. And who knows? If your character gets popular enough, you'll start getting good film offers again," he added, bringing Paritosh's mug back within his reach, sensing that his client's anger had dissipated and there was only a bit of doubt surrounding him.

"Let me check with Debolina," Paritosh said, "see if she's okay with living in Delhi again. I'll have to ask the kids, too. They were born here; they've lived here their whole lives, and I don't think they'll be okay moving to a new place."

But then, when he told them of Lalit's plan, all three of their faces lit up, and Debolina instantly called up her parents in Delhi to announce their imminent arrival. His daughters—Nandini was 10 at that time, and Indrani was 12—were not one bit sad about leaving Bombay, and were looking forward to meeting their grandparents. He'd often find them conspiring with Debolina, making plans of places they could visit, of things they could do, and how many new friends they were going to make at the new school.

But Paritosh, who'd left home at the age of 17 to become an actor in Bombay, felt a bit defeated going back to where he grew up. Ironically, he couldn't go back to his actual childhood home—his parents had sold it off to buy a flat in Salt Lake in West Bengal, in an effort to go back to their roots and live among close and distant relatives.

Paritosh couldn't help but focus on one little difference

between their situations. While his parents' move was a dream come true and was driven by choice, his could only be categorised as a nightmare—a last-ditch effort to save his career.

Paritosh frowns as he stares at the screen, clutching the remote tighter in his grip. He's forgotten all about the young man who is jumping through fires and jumping across buildings in front of him. His mind is full of the days he spent on *Dilli ki Rooh*'s set.

There was a different dynamic at play there. There was a certain kinship amongst the actors, the directors, and the rest of the crew that went beyond inside jokes and familiarity. And try as he might, Paritosh just didn't feel like he was one of them. Even when they tried to help him, suggest ways in which he could enhance his performance—add more melodrama to his acting—it felt like he was being singled out, and being told that he wasn't good enough for them. He resented them, to be sure, and that feeling only grew as he spent more and more days with them, until . . .

He gets up from the sofa, feeling the lingering irritation from those days warm his blood. He looks around his room in annoyance, feeling the need for something strong to calm his nerves, and then walks with purpose into the dining room. He's way past the kitchen, on his way to his bedroom when he stops and ponders what he's about to do.

He reminds himself of the promise he'd made to Debolina, that he wouldn't touch a drink in her absence. Not after last time, when he lost his job on *Dilli ki Rooh* and passed out on the sofa. She and the kids were away then as well, and came home to him lying still on the floor with blood on his forehead. Indrani and Nandini screamed, fearing him dead, but Debolina knew with one whiff of the air around him that he was drunk and must have stumbled and banged his head on a side table.

"Ki holo, Paritosh?" she asked, seething underneath. *What happened, Paritosh?*

"Jaani na," he replied. *Don't know.*

When he sobered up, he told her then that it wasn't truly his fault, that sometimes when he drank too much, he lost a little control. And that he would be more careful from thereon. But she still threw out his entire stash and gave him a look that said it was the last straw. One more mistake and he knew she would leave him.

No, he thinks, as he enters his bedroom, he won't make the same mistake again. He'll only have one glass of whisky, and stop right there. He has a Blenders Pride inside his wardrobe, hidden beneath piles of clothes he never wears. He takes those shirts out now. He wants to savour the moment, to make the feeling last. Having placed his clothes on the bed, he gently takes out a worn, hole-ridden grey sweater, cradling it in his arms like a baby. He unravels the woollen garment carefully, relishing the softness of the yarn, and then looks at the bottle in the dying sunlight shining into the room.

"I'll only have the one glass," he repeats out loud.

His eyes feel heavy even though he hasn't opened them yet. And there is a pain behind his eyes that makes him wish he were dead. But his throat is dry and rough, he needs water. And he must get up from the sofa to the fridge. So he half opens his eyes, stands up, stumbles a bit, and moves in the general direction of the kitchen.

He yawns as he opens the fridge and takes a bottle of water out, drinking it entirely in one go. And then lets out a sigh of contentment as his brain begins to wake up. He scrunches and opens his eyes as he waddles back to the living room, only to stop dead next to his sofa chair. Eyes open wide, he stares at the large crack on the television screen.

Did I do that? he thinks. *But how? With what?*

The bottle of Blenders Pride is still on the table. It's completely empty, but undamaged. He can't think of anything else he could have used as a projectile, so he walks up to the TV, slowly and with purpose, and takes a look at the screen. He can't see what would have caused such an injury, there's nothing on the floor but shards of glass and a few pieces of plastic. It is only when he looks around, to check whether any of the showpieces have been hurt, that he finds the remote control next to a dolphin on the lowest shelf. It must have struck the screen and bounced off to land perfectly by the crystals.

As he picks it up in his hand, the phone begins to ring and he jumps back in alarm at the sudden intrusion. For a moment he's afraid that it's Debolina on the line, calling him with the news that they were going to return early—in an hour or so. But when he picks up the phone, it's Lalit he hears on the other side.

"Paritosh?"

"Yes," he tries, but it comes out reeking of sandpaper. "Yes?" he tries again.

"Don't tell me you're ill."

"No. It's just . . . nothing. Why are you calling me?"

"Because your shoot is in two hours? I reminded you yesterday, before you asked me about the possibility of getting a film role." Lalit sounds a bit angry and a bit tired.

"Oh, the light bulb company." He rubs his eyes with a hand and yawns widely.

"Yes, the light bulb company. The shoot is at Daryaganj, right outside Ramjas Bicycle Repairs. I gave you the directions yesterday. But I can tell you again, if you want?"

"No. I remember. I mean, I have the paper somewhere . . . I wrote it down . . . I just need to find it."

"Paritosh?" Lalit sounds sad now.

"I'll find it, don't worry."

"No. It's not that." He sighs. "You're not the first one with this . . . problem. Practically everyone I work with indulges in . . . something from time to time."

"I know."

"But you have trouble controlling it."

"I know." He stares at the TV.

"Do you remember what happened at the set of *Dilli ki Rooh*?"

"I said I was sor . . ."

"You arrived drunk at the set and then threw the bottle at the director."

"And I was deeply apologetic the next day."

"You kept cursing at him and the others—the actors, the

make-up artists, the spot boys. You said you were better than them, and that they were all jealous of you and were conspiring against you."

Paritosh sighs but it turns into a yawn. "I remember," he says, voice still rough.

"Are you sure? Then why do you sound like you're head-numbingly hungover? How will you ever go back to films if you can't get a grip over your drinking habit?"

"It's not a *habit*, Lalit. I rarely ever drink and sometimes . . ."

"Does Debolina know?"

"No. She isn't here. The kids aren't here either."

"Is it Blenders Pride? I know I shouldn't have booked that ad for you, shouldn't have fallen for your promises that you wouldn't drink again."

"Listen, Lalit," Paritosh says now, having finally brought his voice to its normal tone. "I'm totally fine. I only had a few glasses, nothing more. And right now it's getting late; I need to head out for the shoot. So . . . I'll talk to you later?" He presents his statement as a question, but doesn't wait for an answer.

As he places the receiver back into its cradle, he considers calling up Debolina and telling her the truth, or at least a version of it—that he accidentally broke the television set. His hand hovers over the receiver in indecision, before Paritosh completely moves away from the phone and heads back to his room to dress for the shoot.

More than anything, he's glad his family isn't here to witness his little hiccups.

Yesterday, when she and the kids were getting ready to leave, Debolina asked if he wanted to come along. He was invited to her parents' place, as well, she reminded him. But he refused to go. He was tired, he'd told her, of listening to her father tell him he should leave his "unstable profession" and join their business of Bengali saris, even though Debolina herself had recently joined her father as an associate.

"And anyway," he said, "I have a shoot in Daryaganj around the same time. I can't miss that out."

"Is that the truth or are you just going to stay home and glare at the TV?" she wondered.

"Can't it be both?" he answered with a tentative smile.

<hr>

His eyes are still warm and tired from the hangover when he parks his white Maruti 800 in Daryaganj an hour later. He's found a little alley to keep his car in, leaving practically no space between the walls of a house and the passenger side of his car, on the left. He has brought his television with him, figuring he'll find someone to fix it for him here, or nearby, in Chandni Chowk. He has his glasses with him, just in case he finds it difficult to read the script. He's given his hair the one-comb-over. And he is dressed in a pair of dark blue trousers, a white shirt, and his whisky-scented grey sweater—it's a bit chilly this November morning. His shoes, once white, are dark and murky, and veering on total collapse. The sole on the left, glued up last month, is already starting to flap about with every forward step.

Somehow he gets through with the shoot. He is supposed to play the role of a tired, dull man, so the entire hungover look actually works in his favour, though the director keeps ordering the spot boy to give him cups of tea between breaks. He says his lines, acts in as many shots as the director wants, he poses for the print ads as well—but he remembers nothing of the script as he leaves the premises and heads out to look for someone to repair the TV.

It's evening now, as he crosses over to Chandni Chowk looking for a shop that might help him. He is just about to give up when he sees 'Repair Services' on the other side of the road. The building, he notes, looks like it belongs in a play. There is a set-like quality to it, and he is reminded for a brief moment of a school production, where much of the first act took place outside a shop that looked just like this one. The walls look two-dimensional, like they could just fold into smaller shapes at the end of the day, to be put away in a storage room. And the board itself, which declares 'Repair Services', looks as if it's been manufactured to look that way—dusty and old. Still he walks, a bit intrigued to be honest, and steps inside the shop.

"Hello," a woman calls out to him. She is behind the counter, on the right. Paritosh nods at her as he looks around. Behind her, and elsewhere in the little room, are shelves and shelves full of antiques and odd objects.

Again the thought hits him that it is all staged. Everything seems to be placed in just the right place. Each item in the shop has a role to play. The grandfather clock is both a monument to time as well as artistry; the teapots are so intricately painted over that they look like pieces of art; and then there's the wooden door at the back of the room—it looks nondescript and dull, but there is a certain power around it. If the whole place were a stage, it's from there that the players would enter and exit.

The moment he thinks so, the door itself opens up and an old man, dressed in white, comes out of it. His face is clean-shaven and wise, and his hair is combed back and carefully styled. On his nose is a pair of dainty silvery glasses, which he now pushes back closer to his eyes.

"How can I help you?" he asks, coming to stand next to the woman, who is dressed in a yellow salwar kameez with a white cardigan on top of it.

"It's my television," Paritosh begins, as he takes the four steps to the counter. "Someone . . . ah . . . my daughters accidentally broke the screen, and I was wondering . . . would it be possible to fix it?"

"Of course, it'll be no problem at all," the bespectacled man says immediately.

"Are you sure?" Paritosh asks. "You haven't even seen it . . ."

"Then bring it here," the man cuts in. "I'll wait."

"We close the shop at seven," the woman contributes. "And it's only five now."

It takes a while for Paritosh to take the TV out of his car—someone has parked a motorcycle right beside the driver side—but thankfully it's a small TV, only 18 inches wide, and it isn't that heavy either, so he manages to carry the device all the way back to the shop. A man comes out of nowhere and helps him the last few metres to the shop. He leaves just as suddenly, mumbling something about the time not being right, confusing Paritosh to no end.

Once inside, the old man quickly takes over the TV, instructing Paritosh to place it inside his workshop—through the teak door. And he's left talking to the woman behind the counter. Her name is Jaya, she tells him. "And you're Paritosh Mukherjee, aren't you?" she asks.

"I . . . uh. Yes," he says. It's been a while since someone's recognised him, and he is a bit flabbergasted to think of a proper response.

"My Dadaji," she points at the workshop, "recognised you right away. He said you worked in films. But I couldn't recall any of them . . . and then I remembered, there was a show of yours I used to watch . . . *Dilli* something."

"*Dilli ki Rooh,*" he tiredly responds.

"That's right." Her face lights up. "But you left the show, didn't you?"

He sighs. "I did." He looks at the clock behind him, on the wall. He wonders how long this will take.

"Oh, why is that?" she asks.

"Creative differences," he says, and she finally catches on and starts talking about something else—about the history of Chandni Chowk. He can tell she is excited about the topic, but he only nods along once in a while. His mind is elsewhere, his mood is off.

Back inside his house, the first thing he does—even before he installs the television once again—is detach the phone line from his telephone. He doesn't want to take a potential call from Lalit, or anyone for a while. He turns on the newly-furbished

TV though. The other option, of being alone with his thoughts, is too much.

The first thing he sees on the screen is another episode of *Dilli ki Rooh*. It looks like they are playing an old one, back from when he had not been fired yet. A part of him wants to switch off the TV right then, but another part of him—the one that's greedy—wants him to bask in his acting talents. And then there's the fact that he has no recollection of ever filming this scene, where he's reacting to a dialogue his "younger brother" is delivering to his "child".

"That's strange," he says at the same time his character speaks those very words on the show. He jumps back on his sofa as his on-screen character pushes back on his chair.

"That's not possible," they both say. "What's happening?"

Both versions of Paritosh look around, trying to see if the other actors have noticed the otherworldly phenomenon. They wait for a second or two, but when there is no exclamation of surprise from the "younger brother" and the "child", who are just getting on with their dialogues, the Paritosh in his sofa-seat decides to experiment with his situation a bit more.

He closes his eyes and pushes the buttons for a random number on the remote, leaving everything to chance, and finds himself as an anchor inside a newsroom. He's dressed in a dark blue suit, with a black tie; his hair is combed perfectly—with a left parting—and he can even see cufflinks, silver and shining, near his wrists. There is a white table in front of him, bearing only a thin, blank paper on it. Behind him, as the backdrop, is a view of the Worli Sea Face, where he would often take to walking when he lived in Bombay.

There's a newsflash on the top, in yellow lettering, which reads, "Paritosh Mukherjee has just realised what his TV can do". Beneath it, on the right, in black, next to Paritosh himself, is an inset window that proclaims: "He can't decide if he's losing his mind or if this is actually happening to him." And then, both the newsflash and the inset, and even the backdrop, changes to display just one simple question: "What are you going to do about it?"

His heart is thumping so wildly that he can hear it in his ears, and he is so shocked that he is gripping the arms of the sofa (the chair on the television), frozen in one place, not knowing what exactly he should do.

"Oh," the inset window reads a second later. "Looks like he's going to pick up the remote again."

His hands are shaking as he changes the channels—he's the batsman at a live cricket game, and the bowler as well. When he hits the ball high in the air, and a fieldsman catches it, near the boundary line, he is the player and the hordes of crowd. Another press of a button and he is in a jungle, in search of a tigress and her cubs. Another press and he is cooking a dish in front of him. Another press and he is being shot by a villain. Another press and is singing a song in an auditorium.

In some channels there is only one of him, in others there are several clones that seem to be aping his every move. And in every changed scenario, he feels a change inside him as well. He can feel the presence of hitherto unknown knowledge in his system. He can recognise ingredients he hasn't heard of, he can remember dialogues he's never said, and he can understand the trail marks of wild animals as if it's second nature to him.

As exhilarating as the feeling is, as the revelation is, he feels scared as well. This is an entirely unknown territory and he has no idea how to traverse it. In one instant he switches off the television, hoping all will be well. But when he turns it back on, it's him as the news anchor on screen again.

"Newsflash," it says above him. "You're not handling this very well, are you?"

The two versions of Paritosh shake their heads in "no".

Letters appear in the inset window: "Well, then, why don't you head to settings?"

He frowns. As far as he can remember, the settings are quite basic—one to adjust the brightness, another to sharpen or dull the scenes, and another to change the colour tone of the picture. There is no such setting to adjust what's happening to him. At least, that was the case the last time he checked.

But now when he presses the button for 'settings', right below 'brightness' is a section called 'perspective'. He selects the option and feels the very atoms that make up his being vibrate with purpose. They are jumping inside him, preparing to move. And then a second later he feels a shot of pain pass through his brain and his nasal cavity and out his nostrils. He swims through the air like an arrow towards the television set, and then he's wearing the news anchor's clothes—a blue jacket on top of a beige sweater vest. He looks around, but there are no cameras around him. The room he's in is shaped exactly like his television set, with three walls being the news studio. But the fourth, the one right ahead of him, is more of a window to the outside world.

It's there his sight lingers, where his unmoving body now

lies on the sofa. His head is lolled to the side, his eyes open wide in shock, and his fingers loose around the remote. He tries hard, using his TV hands, to try and pick up the remote and change the setting, or do anything to the real him. He runs up to the window and hits the glass with his fists. But still, nothing happens. And even as he keeps muttering "no" with increasing despair, his lifeless hand falls open and the remote falls to the ground, landing on the power button.

—————•—————

It takes a while for the TV to be switched on again. Two days, in fact. And it only happens because Indrani can't stand being alone with her thoughts. She turns on the TV, hoping not to see one of her father's films on screen. She doesn't know what she would do if that were to happen. But then the screen comes to life, opens to a news channel, and it's her Papa in the anchor's seat.

"Please don't turn off the television, Indrani," he says. "It's really me. This is not some trick."

She stares at him for a long time, before she attempts in a small voice: "But . . . but you're in the hospital. I just saw you there . . . an hour ago."

"So I'm not dead?"

"You're in a coma."

"Oh. That's good . . . I guess." Already he feels a bit detached from the body he used to have. Inside the TV he is a floating being. He has fingers and toes, and ears and nose. But he can't really feel them. There is no sensation.

"Why is the box next to you saying I should call Mumma and Nandini here?" Indrani wonders.

"It is? Then you should do that."

His wife runs in first, and her momentary look of shock is followed by a tired question.

"Ki holo, Paritosh?" she asks.

"Jaani na," he replies.

When Nandini too is in the room, he explains what has happened. And they rush to go to the settings and get him back, but there is no way to change it. His daughters and wife try their best; they even switch the TV on and off multiple times, but nothing happens. Later, they try to find the shop he had gone to, but they are unable to find it. Paritosh can't recall the name of the place, and there are so many buildings in Chandni Chowk that Debolina and his daughters feel like they are getting lost in a maze when they go on their search.

"So what should we do?" his wife asks after several failed attempts.

"Well, why don't you tell me about your day?" he answers.

And so it begins, their new routine. On weekdays, he gets switched on at 3pm, when his daughters come back from school, and gets powered down at 10pm, at bedtime. On weekends the opening time shifts from 3 pm to 12 but the closing hour stays the same.

When they need to talk to him face-to-face, they go to the news channel. The inset windows and the newsflash ticker help with the conversation, too. But other times, they take him to cooking shows, to documentaries, to cricket matches, and even mythological shows. It's a game for his daughters, to have their father go through these things. They make him walk for hours in the Gobi desert, a tiring exercise even for him, but he bears it with a grin to see his daughters enjoy the visuals so much. And when their Papa complains or, at times, scolds them, they just mute him. His wife does that on some occasions too. Like when he objects to getting a loan from her father to pay for his hospital bills, she frowns at him as he traverses the jungles of South America.

"Well, then, what do you suggest?" she asks him. "Are *you* going to pay for it somehow?"

She doesn't wait for an answer from him, instantly muting him and leaving the room altogether in her anger.

———◦———

There are times when he is made speechless by choice, too. The first time is when they tell him, on the very first day, that Lalit had tried calling him several times to give him some good news—a lead role for Paritosh in an art-house movie—but had found the telephone engaged.

The second time is when, three months after the "incident", they address him as a team. He can tell even before they open their mouths that they want to discuss an uncomfortable subject, so he braces for the worst. But what they tell him is:

"We are getting another television set."

"What do you mean? I . . . I'm here . . . How can you?"

"We mean no disrespect, Papa, but it's really weird to see you in every film or show we watch. We don't even get to hear all the dialogues with you talking over them. It . . . it gets a bit annoying," Indrani says.

Nandini adds, "Remember the last time we went to the Royale Palace, and you talked so much that others kept shushing you?"

"I think a second TV will be good for all of us," his wife says, her words final. And Paritosh looks on, trying to control his emotions, trying to understand why his family would do such a thing. It is the oddest feeling in the world, to feel jealous of a machine.

"But then," he asks, "I don't understand . . . where will I go?"

"Right here, beside us," his wife says, pointing to the space between the two sofa chairs where a tall table has been placed. "We've talked to an electrician and he'll fix everything tomorrow."

He doesn't know what to say then; the cauliflower florets he'd been frying on the stove, to show his girls a new recipe, had now burnt to a crisp. And there's nothing to do but for him to throw it in the dustbin.

———o———

Days go by just like this, and he settles into his new position in the room and their lives. His eyesight is much better from inside the TV, sharp and defined. He can see things quite clearly inside the room. From where they have placed him, he can see the clock, too. He can see the time as it starts to creep towards

10 o'clock. And he waits. He knows his wife and children will start to yawn, and reason with him that they need their rest for office and school tomorrow. Sometimes, he can feel a sense of irritation from them, too; the desire in them to say he wouldn't understand, not anymore. He doesn't have to get up in the morning, work the entire day, only to feel tired and drained at night. They never say that, but he can tell they are thinking it.

And still, he can't help it. When the time arrives, nearly every night, he pleads with them to stay a bit longer. "If you start to fall asleep on the couch I'll wake you up," he says.

"Papa, it won't be good for my back," Indrani says, who is already so grown-up at 12.

"And tomorrow's a Saturday, so we'll switch you on at midday. We'll have more time together then," Nandini adds.

"Yes, why don't you rest a while, Paritosh," his wife opines, walking towards him. "And we'll meet each other fresh-faced tomorrow."

He gives them a reassuring smile and braces himself for the push of the button. They don't know, because he has not told them, what happens after they switch him off. It had been in the early days when his kids had asked him, when they were still a bit scared, and he hadn't wanted to upset them. He hadn't wanted to cause Debolina any pain, either. So when they had asked him what he did after the TV got switched off, he said he just slept off. That his consciousness went into a state of pause, and he had dreams just like they did.

In reality, it's a different matter. Every night, after his family goes off to sleep, he roams around in the vast, dark emptiness inside the television set and waits out till either his wife or children switch him back on. Sometimes, if he really strains his audio capabilities, he can hear them leave the house in the morning.

Turn Up The Radio (Only) When It Rains

The balcony is her favourite place in the flat. Here, Inaya sits down in her decades-old sofa chair, a book in hand, and whiles away her time at home. Earlier, when she was still married, before she had parted ways with Bhaskar, amicably, he would also join her outside. He would listen to classical music and she would focus on her novels. The sounds never bothered her, she welcomed them. And even now, having retired a few months ago, at the age of 60, she prefers the open company of her balcony, from where she can hear her entire neighbourhood. She welcomes the noisy cars, the snatches of conversations from the flat beside her own, and most of all the chattering of rain during the Monsoon.

It's only the beginning now, only a few days into June, and the greys in the sky are sparse. But she can smell the rain in the air, the promise of drenched earth, which fills her up with an unexplained joy. It makes her want to seek out more books she hasn't read yet, even though there are many in all the nooks and crannies inside her flat. Also, her brain rationalises, it's been a few months since she's left her housing society in Noida, so preoccupied has she been, lately, with settling into life after retirement.

There is no choice; really, she *has* to visit the Sunday book market in Daryaganj.

———◦———

There are books everywhere at the Sunday market—inside actual shops, or on the pavements, spilling onto the roads. Some are pirated, and you can tell they are so by the quality of the paper used, while the rest are legal copies—new and second-hand. And they are piled up high, in mismatched towers, uncaring whether they have something in common or not, or they are laid out low, in rows, on the ground. There's not much order this way either, but it's easier to pick up a book and look at the back of it without fearing a Jenga-like collapse.

Inaya remembers that one time when she was here with Bhaskar. He had gone off to look for some old records, and as she had turned around to look at him, distracted by his frame walking away, she had accidentally pulled away a book from the middle of a pile and dismantled the entire tower.

She is careful not to repeat that now, as she points at a children's book in the middle of a high-rise pile. If she's not mistaken, she first read this novel when she was eight years old. But she needs to read the synopsis just to be sure.

"I don't think you'll like this one," the bookseller, Jatin, says, as he blows the dust off the novel and pats it with a thud before handing it to her. "You're not old enough to read it," he adds, straight-faced.

She chortles as she browses the jacket, hoping to rekindle a lost memory. The pages rustle as she opens the book further and brings it closer to her nose to breathe in a healthy dose of ink and paper.

"I was waiting for you to do that," Jatin says, and Inaya beams at him.

She's known Jatin for a long time, since he was a young child, helping his father take care of their business. She knows most of the booksellers—Ali, Kaushik, Omar, and the lot, all of whom are in their 30s—and they know her, too. Sometimes they have a better inkling of what she would like to read and what she won't.

"What do you suggest?" she asks, returning the book to Jatin.

He makes a show of thinking hard, scratching his scruffy chin, and then frowning in thought, before he snaps his fingers and tells her he has an idea. But she'll have to follow him to another shop. "I don't know if you've been there before," he adds.

"Well, what is it?" she asks.

Jatin looks at Omar, another bookseller, tells him to keep a watch on his books, and asks her to follow him. They only stroll a small distance before they come to stand before an antique shop. Jatin catches the owner's attention; a middle-aged man named Joy, who has an impressive moustache, curling at the tips, and asks him to get "that item".

The man's eyes light up and he walks farther into the shop, which is not only filled with history but also smells like it, with all the dust and rust in the air. The walls are devoted to old family photos, of varying lengths, where people are sitting in the living room, on and around an ornate sofa, in ornate, traditional clothes themselves; or are out in a garden, sitting on plastic chairs in a circle, wearing formal clothing to suit both Western and Indian sensibilities; or are in the mountains, somewhere, dressed in sweaters and mufflers, the ground beneath their feet covered with pinecones. Only a few of them are in colour; largely they are a mix of black and white, and sepia.

There are cupboards and tables on either side of the shop, leaving a narrow path into the storage room, where Joy has gone looking for her gift. The cupboards are stuffed and promise to hold memories as well, but the tables are gleaming with silver and gold, and it's towards them that Inaya's attention is drawn.

There are hookahs of all kinds, each with their own burden of rust to carry; some, she knows, could go all the way back to the medieval times, when the Mughals ruled Delhi. She picks a small silver one, tarnished in places, with her hands and brings it closer to her eyes. This one, she is sure, must have belonged to someone important.

Jatin guffaws from the edge of the shop, leaning against the doorframe. He has been looking at the wares as well, but with a sort of lazy interest, certainly not with the intention to buy one in the future. He keeps his voice to a whisper, to ensure Joy can't overhear them, and advises her not to believe him if he says the hookahs belonged to Shah Jahan, the Mughal emperor who built the Taj Mahal. "He has sold countless hookahs by saying so. And has charged thousands of rupees in the process." He grins. "Most of these customers were foreigners, though. And they could afford it," he adds, and then immediately straightens up when he sees Joy emerge from the storage room.

Inaya turns her head around to see what the owner is

carrying and is more than a little surprised at the sight. Held in his arms, cradled like a baby, is a wooden Murphy radio from the 1960s.

There's some space on the hookah table, near where Inaya is standing, and he places the radio over there, gently, so as not to disturb its internal components. And Jatin, realising the moment has come, walks over to them and tells her that they—all the booksellers—wanted to give her a retirement gift, something that would keep her engaged much like a story would. "But we had no idea what exactly to give to you, until one day Joy joined us during an afternoon tea break, and told us he'd recently acquired this radio," he says, placing a hand on the said device.

"A gift?"

She had expected the vinyl recording from Bhaskar, where he was playing the violin; and she had an inkling that the teachers at Wisdom Public School, her former place of work, would present her with a Kindle and a Bengali sari (which turned out to be a lovely pink and blue Taant, bought from a local sari shop). She had even known that her next-door neighbours would send her a bouquet (of daffodils) and a box of sweets, but she hadn't expected this. At all.

"But . . ." she starts, when Jatin interrupts. "You've bought so many books from us over the years, Madam. This is the least we could do."

"I just . . . don't know what to say. Thank you. I had no idea . . . and just, thank you."

"You're welcome," Jatin says, and then shifts focus to Joy. "Tell her how you acquired it."

The antique collector nods, and begins: "One day a man

came to me, and told me he had found a room full of such things in his ancestral home. And now that he was selling the house itself, he wanted to get rid of things he could not distribute among his siblings."

"What else did he give you?" Inaya asks.

"Rugs, telephones, tea sets—all sorts of things. They are all over the shop now," he says, and then points to a sepia-toned photo on the wall to their right. "That's him," he points to a young boy in a long-sleeved t-shirt and a pair of shorts, scowling, cross-legged on the ground in a garden, as his family members sit above him, in chairs. "He said he was angry because he wanted to sit on a chair, but there weren't enough of them," Joy adds, laughing, as Jatin chuckles.

But Inaya feels differently. "I would have kept a photo like that," she half-wonders, feeling a pang of sudden, sad nostalgia for a family she has never met.

"You can buy it, if you want?" Joy suggests.

"No," she says, shaking her head. And then adds, "Who buys these, anyway? Does the original owner ever come back?"

"Sometimes, yes. But a lot of people come here looking for a photo of a family member, especially if they used to live here a long time ago. And then there are others, who are either researchers, or those who consider these to be like any other picture, or a painting, who buy it to add character to their walls."

"A few years ago," Jatin says, carrying the radio in his hands, on their short walk to the book market, "Omar sold you a book about radios. Do you remember that?"

"I . . . yes, I do," she says. "I told him my grandparents used to have one. That when I was a child I used to spend hours listening to it while reading books. But," she adds, turning her head to look at him, "I'm surprised Omar recalled that interaction."

"It's our job, Madam," he says, as they reach the part of the market Jatin, Omar, and others occupy. "To note down every little thing a customer says. You never know what might help us sell a book."

"But we aren't selling anything here," Omar adds, coming to stand next to Jatin. Ali and Kaushik don't leave their stalls as they have customers to cater to, but they watch the interaction with interest. "This is our retirement gift to you. Jatin told you that, didn't he?" He looks at the man in question.

"He did, and he told me that you were the one to suggest it," Inaya says.

"Oh, that was nothing," Omar replies.

"I don't think so, and to buy such a costly thing . . ." Inaya says.

"It wasn't that expensive," Jatin steps in. "And, you see, one of the dials is . . ."

". . . missing," Omar finishes sheepishly.

"It works perfectly well other than that, though," Jatin quickly adds.

They seem a bit worried she'll feel disrespected on receiving a broken gift, but she appreciates the history behind the radio, and the fact they made an effort to buy a thoughtful present for her. She tells them the same, and waves a "thanks" to Kaushik and Ali as well. And then she asks where she could get the radio repaired, if there was a place nearby.

"You will find one in Chandni Chowk," Omar says, "but if not there, then there is Nehru Place. You'll most definitely find a repair shop for a radio over there."

It's only when she's deep inside the lanes of Chandni Chowk that she realises she had forgotten to buy a book from them. But then again, it would have been extremely difficult for her to carry a radio as well as a bag of novels. As it is, she is finding it a bit awkward to manage the radio in her arms. It's not so heavy that she can't carry it, but it's definitely cumbersome.

She is ready to take a break and place the radio on the pavement for a while, when she notices a board across the road, which tells her she's looking straight at a repair shop. Relieved, she checks both sides of the oncoming traffic, and carves a path through the people, cycles, and cars on the road. She's lucky that there is a bit of traffic jam up ahead, so she can move in between stalled vehicles.

She gives the exterior a cursory look, noticing only that the two-storied building is old and the two windows need a bit of cleaning. There's a hazy look to them caused by a gathering of dust on their surfaces. The door is open and at once she is in another world. The antique shop was nothing compared to this one, where each and every corner has been filled up with devices

and gadgets, broken and whole. And even a grandfather clock—
simple in its details but magnificent in its presence. There is a
ceiling fan right at the centre of the space, a solitary presence in
the entire shop, which is moving its blades leisurely, squeaking at
an interval of five seconds. She stands under it, craving the relief
from humidity it provides, but still fearing it might come apart,
like a deadly Frisbee.

"It won't fall on your head," a voice on her right tells her.

Inaya looks at the source of reassurance—a woman in her
40s, dressed in a blue sari with yellow horses on it, her hair tied
up in a neat bun. The bindi at the centre of her forehead is an
electric blue, just about matching the shade of her sari. She is
sitting behind a glass-top counter, with only her head and shoulders visible. There is a table fan on the counter, to her left, facing
her, threatening to undo her bun. Indeed, a few wisps of hair
have already let loose and are flying around her serpent-like.

"I know," Inaya says, laughing. "But you can't help but
wonder, sometimes."

The sari-clad woman stands up, smiling. "I've had that fear,
too, but Dadaji told me not to worry, he is very careful about
maintaining the shop." She points at the wooden door at the
back of the store, towards the left. "He's in there now, talking to
a friend. He'll be back soon." She curiously looks at the radio in
Inaya's arms, and then looks up at her face. "Is something wrong
with it?"

"Well, yes. Actually, I don't know." Inaya finally moves
from beneath the fan and places the radio on the counter
between them. "I retired a few months ago, and the booksellers
at Daryaganj gave this to me, as a gift."

"I've known them for a long time, you see," Inaya adds, seeing the confused expression on the other woman's face. "They knew I used to love listening to the radio as a child, and they bought this for me keeping that in mind." Her voice catches as she says the last few words. Saying what they did out loud makes Inaya realise how lovely their effort had been.

"What a wonderful thing to do," the woman across the counter half-whispers. "Aajkal itna kaun sochta hai?" she wonders. *Whoever is this thoughtful these days?*

"That's true," Inaya responds, shaking her head in affirmation.

"Jaya? Are you there?" a man enquires from the other side of the workshop door before it opens and a white-haired, bespectacled old man steps out. He looks to be in his late 70s at the least, and yet, there is an ease to the way he walks towards them which belies his age.

He stops near the door, and Inaya can see quite an evident difference in the length of his arms. She thinks of all the bullying he might have faced in life, especially in his younger years, and her heart sinks a bit. Children can be very cruel—she has seen so herself at school—and she hopes that this joyful old man before her hasn't suffered at the hands of bullies.

"Sorry, I'll be with you soon," he says. "I didn't realise a customer was here." He turns around to face the younger man behind him, who looks to be around 40. He's in a pair of navy trousers and a white shirt, all of which clashes with the oddly-shaped pair of neon green running shoes he's sporting on his feet. On his arm, wrapped around his wrist, is one of those fancy smartwatches that tells you everything from the weather to your heart rate.

She can't hear what the two are talking about, their voices are so low, so she turns her attention back to the counter and the woman she now knows is named Jaya.

"Do you know how to operate this radio?" she asks. "As in, is there anything else to do beyond turning the dials this way and that?" She chuckles.

"I don't think there is," Jaya answers, smiling. "But I'm sure there'll be tutorials on YouTube, anyway. I mean, everything is . . ." she derails, taking a moment to wave goodbye to the green-shoed man, who is on his way out.

"I apologise once again," the old man tells Inaya as he moves from the main door to the counter. "I think I lost track of time talking to an old friend."

"Oh, sure. No problem," she says. "I've only just walked into the shop, anyway."

"Really?" he says, finally behind the counter, next to Jaya. "Now, what do we have here . . . Oh, is this is a 1962 Murphy radio?" He picks it up with both hands and looks it over, his glasses sliding down on his nose. "And it looks to be in good condition, too. Just hasn't been used much in the last few years. Oh," he adds, as he places the radio back on the counter to push his glasses back, "I see that it's missing a dial. You'll want to fix that?"

"Yes, thank you," Inaya says. "And, also, could you please check and see if it's actually working? If any parts need to be replaced, or if something needs to be repaired."

"Sure, of course," he answers.

Jaya jumps in then, contributing the fact that it's Inaya's retirement gift, and that she used to work in a school.

"You must feel relieved to have peace and quiet again," the old man says, guffawing.

Inaya smiles in return. "To be honest," she says, "I actually miss the noise a bit."

Dadaji gives her an odd look. "I know what you mean," he says, before patting the radio. "Well, I'm sure this will help you from now on."

She nods. "I hope so too."

"Hmmm," he says, pausing, staring at the radio. "Say, why don't you come back tomorrow? Around this time, 10:30 in the morning, and I'll have this ready for you."

Inaya agrees, glad that she is retired and doesn't have to go to school on Monday mornings. She offers to pay half of the estimated cost of services, which the old man speculates to be Rs 300, but he refuses, telling her that he'll wait until tomorrow.

True to his word, the radio is functional and ready for her the next day. She doesn't spend much time at the shop this time, her excitement making her want to rush to her flat and try out the radio for herself. But she is sure to profusely thank the old man and his granddaughter, and to pay them Rs 100 more than the agreed price.

In the Delhi metro, on the way home, she sits inside the women's-only compartment, having found a seat a few stations away from Chandni Chowk, at Rajiv Chowk. She places the device in her lap, stares at it with a little smile on her face, resolving to look for an instrumental-only station, if there is one in existence. It's been a while since she's listened to a transistor radio, and she is not sure what she'll find in there.

Once home, she is really tired from the journey—of walking in the heat and of travelling in the metro, changing trains at one place—but still she places her prized possession on the centre table in her living room, and switches it on. From her right, where her balcony is situated, she can hear the soft rumblings of thunder, the hesitant rainfall of the initial Monsoon clouds. She takes it as a good omen, and begins her search.

She spends several minutes that way, leaning into the radio, on the lookout for something that would catch her attention. But all she hears are ads. Hardly anywhere does she come across an actual song. Even when she, accidentally, comes upon the voice of the RJ, it's because he or she is playing a prank on an unsuspecting member of the public, who has been set up by someone in their own family or friends circle. The whole thing is tedious, and Inaya starts to lose interest in the beautiful transistor, when her hand turns the frequency dial a bit too harshly, and she hears the dying crunch of the spring that controls it.

She lets out a gasp, her fingers still on the dial, when she hears a questioning "hello".

"Is anybody there?" she hears, again. It's a man's voice, someone older.

She is sure she's come across a radio play of some sort, but still she returns a shaky "hi" herself.

A long sigh. The man speaks again: "Oh, good. I've found someone at last."

She sits back straighter in her sofa, away from the transistor, in shock. And then leans into the radio once again. "Is this . . . are you." She tries again. "Can you hear me?"

"Absolutely. I can hear the rain, too."

"But then . . . how is this possible? And . . . and, where are you? *Who* are you?" Nothing in life has prepared Inaya for such a situation, and she is full of questions she has no answers to.

The man laughs—a rich, velvety sound. "Fortunately, I have a reply for each of your queries. How is this possible, you asked? Well, I have this vintage 20th century HAM radio with me, which allows me to have conversations with people around the world, such as yourself. As to where I live, I won't give you my sector code because of safety reasons, but I can tell you that I am a resident of Upper Delhi, in Quadrant IV. And that my name is Orko 23."

She doesn't say anything for a long time, for about five minutes. He thinks the transmission is lagging and does not eke out her response, and she thinks it's one of those pranks that RJs play. She is cautious as she replies to him: "That sounds interesting."

"You don't believe me." Orko chuckles. "You're not from 4016, are you?"

"What is that supposed to mean?"

"Which year is it there?" the man asks.

"2016," she says, getting a bit exasperated, thinking of changing the channel or switching off the radio.

"So you're four years away . . ." he trails off.

"Now what is *that* supposed to mean? Is this is a prank of some sort? Or are you phishing for some sensitive information from me, to hack into my emails and bank account? Because I'm warning you now, I may be old but . . ."

"Hold on, hold on," the man says, "I'm not trying to do any of that. I truly *am* from the future. And I have a way to prove that to you."

"Of course you do."

The man quietly chortles at her snark. "What if I tell you the exact headlines for the next two days? Will you believe me, then?"

"I can't promise."

"Oh, come on. Don't be this way. What do you have to lose?"

It's a week before she decides to talk to him.

She is outside, on the balcony, having spent her entire Sunday listening to the rain, gathering courage to talk to the strange man again.

"Hello," is all she says.

"I had a feeling you would take some time," he answers. "I've heard this is what happens during a time clash, when there is too great a distance between the years of two people, or a group of people."

"Does this happen a lot?" she asks. She is still not quite sure if this is real; and if for a second she thinks something's fishy, she's going to switch off the radio. But for now, she's intrigued. The headlines he had spouted off last Sunday had been accurate word for word.

"I have read about such things happening to people decades or hundreds of years away, but very few have gone the distance we have. People think it's because of the new communications tower on the Moon. It's not only affecting tides, which everyone knew it would do anyway, but it's also causing these cross connections. I think, worldwide, about thirty other people have experienced this. They had these HAM radios, too."

"Funny," she says. "Mine isn't a HAM radio. It's just an ordinary one that catches on a radio station and plays whatever they are broadcasting. And yet . . . I can talk to you."

"It's not an exact science," he chuckles. "I'm not sure how this is working, either."

"You said you're from 4016 . . ."

"I am. But there are so many things I don't know and . . ."

"No. It's not that. I was just wondering why you have any radio at all. I thought such a thing would be defunct by that age."

"You're right. It is. But I'm a fool, you see," he says, smiling. "I've always been fascinated by the past, especially the gadgets and devices people used. Ever since I was a young boy, I used to collect things I'd find at antique shops—everlasting stoves, folding bikes. Even this radio I'm using now was a haul from one of those shops."

"Have you spoken to someone like me before?"

"No. Never. You're the only one."

Her cheeks feel warm. "Can I ask you something else?" This is a question that has been at the back of her mind for a long time now.

"Please, go ahead."

"When you were telling me the headlines, it almost sounded like you had memorised them, that you already *knew*."

He takes a deep breath. "This part is going to seem very odd to you, but please bear with me. And please remember we are a few thousand years away from you."

"Okay"

"You probably have Internet, don't you?" he begins.

"Yes. Of course."

"Well, much in the way you can access the Internet on your mobile phones, we have the same faculty inside our own . . . heads."

A frown takes over her face but he, of course, can't see it, and continues: "The technical term for it is Brain Powering Unit, but we just call it 'mind chip'. All of us are given a choice at the age of 10, and then it's up to us, under parental guidance of course, to accept the implant or reject it and live the kind of life you do, unconnected. But most of us choose to be tethered to each other; it allows us to call or text anyone we want, without ever using an external device. Same with accessing information. We just need to *think* of who we want to call, or what we want to search about, and it'll be pulled up inside our heads."

Her eyebrows rise up and she has the thought that after years of reading novels of all kinds, she is finally experiencing something that could very well fill pages of some sort of sci-fi or speculative book. And so, to drive the narrative forward and to quench her own thirst of inquisitiveness, she asks, "What if you need to show your search results to someone else? Or if there's a message you want someone else to read—how do you do that?"

"We just transmit that onto a nearby surface," he answers. "A table, a wall, the ground."

"And the mind chip . . . Is that why you know so much about us, our way of life?"

"Not exactly. Yes, it is true that I check sources online while talking to you, but I do have an interest in the subject. I'm a historian, you see, and I specialise in ancient technology."

She feels a shiver go down her spine at the mention of "ancient technology", at the fact that she's been dead for thousands of years in his time. But she clears her head of thoughts once again, and pursues another line of questioning.

"Earlier," she says, "you said that I was 'four years away' from something. What was that?"

"Yes, that." He sounds a bit apologetic now, like he doesn't want to answer the question. "That was a bit of a mistake. I shouldn't have said anything, really."

"Is it bad, whatever will happen?"

He sighs. "Yes. A most terrible thing . . . but I don't want to say anything for fear I may cause a chain reaction and affect the course of history. Which is why I also think it's best if I don't look you up online. It's best that neither of us knows. Do you agree?"

"Sure," is all she says, not knowing what else she can say. She has never been the kind who's anxious about the future, never worried over her own mortality, but she is intrigued to say the least. This is a plot twist in their conversation that seems to lie unresolved.

"Oh," Orko says in the silence that follows, "I wasn't accurate before. We haven't done away with every source of information that you use. We still have libraries all over Earth, the very same kind that you use . . . full of paper books. There's one here, too, in Upper Delhi. It's called Inko. It was moved from the Lowers a thousand years ago. Nobody knows who actually founded it, but it still stands even after so many years. I've been there a couple of times myself. Although, to be fair, it's more of a museum; a representation of what your lives used to be like . . . sorry, *are* like."

She doesn't mind that he misspoke. "Tell me more," she says, as the drizzle outside turns to downpour.

And he does, over the course of many days.

He explains the system he had spoken about before, about the Upper and Lower levels that exist in most cities in the world. The villages usually don't have them, he tells her, but he has known of a few in China that do. They even have underground sectors there, in cities like Beijing and Shanghai. In their own country, there are only rumours of a sub-level city, under the Arabian Sea. ("There was a nuclear war scare a hundred years ago and everyone says that's when it was built.")

Although it all seems fantastical to her, she is dismayed too. That even in the future, the world is so divided and disproportionate.

"You thought our time would be more egalitarian?" he asks, fitting into the role of a professor.

"Well . . . yes. I thought at some point, people, the government, would realise . . ."

"I'm sorry, Inaya," he tells her. "But we're not there yet."

Still, he tells her, all's not bad. After all, theirs is a much more organised world, growing out of the need for better planning. Up till then, human civilisation had always been a step away from disorder and turmoil, and people were fed up with overcoming war, health scares, and financial disasters every few years. It was felt that if they were more organised as a species, more in control of the collective resources, then some of the chaotic energy could be diminished. ("That was the beginning of the thought that led to the invention of the Brain Powering Unit.")

This worldwide organisation of people and resources had another side-effect: everyone in the world was assigned a number at birth. The year he was born, there were 30 in total who got to be called Orko. ("Does that mean you were born in the latter half of the year? Maybe somewhere around October?" she asks. "You're absolutely correct," he answers.)

From thereon he progresses to tell her about his personal life, how he was born in an Upper hospital, lived his entire life on that level and only went down for research, for every ancient building was grounded in the Lowers. He became a historian right around the same time he got married. And he was considered an oddball to stick to only one partner throughout his life, before she died fourteen years into marriage. Most people existed inside cohorts, as do his daughters, who are now grown up and have five partners each. ("Our lifestyle must be quite shocking to you," he tells her. "Yes, well," she answers, "it is the future after all.") He didn't marry again, throwing himself into his work. He also began to collect antiques then, even travelling the world to buy some of them. ("I bought this radio at an auction in Inner Rishikesh," he tells her. "What do you mean by 'inner'? Don't tell me people made houses *inside* the mountains, inside the Himalayas?" she asks. "That is exactly what I mean," he answers.)

He tells her he is an old-fashioned man. That while the young ones use the inside of their heads to frame and write thoughts into articles, messages, or documents, he uses the surfaces in front of him to do so. ("It makes me feel like what you must feel, with all the writing you do on your paper and keyboard.")

She tells him about her life, too. She can sense his professional curiosity in some moments; how he is restraining himself from being too intrusive. And she finds it very amusing.

Like him, she was born in Delhi, and got married young, and stayed with that one man her entire life. Bhaskar was much like her, a bit quiet, a bit brooding. And where she found her love in books, he found it in Carnatic music, the traditional music of the south. They never had children, but it was by choice, and they never felt the absence of it once they grew into middle age. The only point of contention, that ripped apart their content life, was Bhaskar's sudden realisation that he wanted more.

"It came out of nowhere, one Saturday morning, while we were sitting on my balcony, but it must have been brewing inside his head for a long time. Anyway," Inaya sighs, "he told me that he wanted to actually learn Carnatic music, that he wanted to go down south to Karnataka, seek the tutelage of a violinist and pursue his dream of becoming a musician. He had worked his entire life in sales and only just realised, in his late 40s, that his life wouldn't be complete if he didn't at least try."

"How is he doing now?" Orko asks.

"Quite well, I think," she answers. "He e-mails me his progress report every once in a while. He's even performed at a concert, in Mumbai. He seems happy, and relieved that his choice was the right one. We're divorced now; it felt like the right thing to do. But we are still friends."

She doesn't tell him how odd she felt at his realisation, and how jealous she sometimes feels of Bhaskar and how he found a new purpose in his life. It isn't like she is dissatisfied with her life. On the contrary, she has done everything she has sought out to do. She can't quite explain it to herself, the ache she sometimes feels when she thinks of Bhaskar and his newfound ambition.

Perhaps Orko senses the disquiet in her, for he remarks, "Do you miss him?"

"No," she answers with determination. "I don't truly miss *him*. I think, after his epiphany, I saw how different we truly were, or had become. But . . . I can't explain it. I think I just miss his company more than anything else."

"I know that feeling," he softly says, and right after, for a blink of a moment, she sees an outline of him on the chair in front of her. She assumes it's him, even though it's only a fuzzy line.

"Did you see something, too?" he asks.

"Yes. What was that?"

"I don't know." There's wonder in his voice that even the thunder outside is unable to drown. "I've never felt anything like this before."

As they head into the months of Monsoon, as every day and night begins to come and go with the outpouring of rain and lightning, and bouts of storms, the faint outline of his shape grows in intensity. There is a greenish tinge to him, which makes her think of the Northern Lights. *There must be something to do with ions and charge and all that,* she thinks. Orko 23 himself seems to think so, though he puts it in much better and detailed sentences than her.

He sees her, too. Sitting across from him. But while she sees him inside her drawing room, he sees her in a fuzzy background that is alien to him. It takes them a few days to realise he is seeing her inside her own drawing room—the years between them doing little to block the view of her sofa, television, tables, plants, and books to his eyes.

———◦———

In the early days, when he is just a haze, he lasts as an image as long as the rain lasts. But later, when their bond goes beyond that of friends, coinciding with his more fleshed-out appearance in Inaya's home, he comes and goes as he wishes.

It is on the day she tells him that she loves him and he says he feels the same way about her, that they finally see each other as they are. They converse as if they are sitting right next to each other, and in a sense, they are. He looks just like she had imagined, with his curly grey hair and smooth-shaved face. He is tall, around six feet in height, and being an old-fashioned man, he wears the kind of clothes that fit right into her time, although his shirt and trousers, owing to the technology of his day, are self-cleaning.

"Has anyone else tried to travel like this? Someone from your time?" she asks one day, when they are in the veranda.

"One of my daughters, Veena 934, tried that when I was speaking to you a few days ago. But even then, only I appeared to you. She stayed at my home."

"What could that mean?"

"I don't know. I really don't. I'll have to look up one of your computers to search now. My little mind chip doesn't work here."

"Do you miss the feeling of being a know-it-all?" she asks, grinning, as he erupts into laughter.

———◇———

This is the way the next few months go by. Every time it rains, he comes along with it. But then the Monsoon comes to an end, and his visits dwindle to stray drizzles that come out of nowhere. His stays last longer because of this, but he always returns to his time.

They enjoy what little time they have together. She shows him her mobile phone and he is so excited to hold it in his hands that he accidentally presses the emergency button a couple of times. They go outside—to the zoo (a concept Orko can't quite grasp), to movie halls (they attend a Paritosh Mukherjee film festival at the Royale Palace), and to monuments that are older than both of them (some haven't survived till Orko's time and he's fascinated to see them). Sometimes they sit in silence too, they watch television (another thing Orko is fascinated by, because he hasn't been able to operate the ones in his collection) or they sit outside and read books.

On days when they can't meet face to face, they spend hours talking on the radio, until one evening, when there is a slow pour outside, he looks at her sadly and she prepares herself for the worst. She had known, she had always known, this wouldn't last.

"What is it?" she asks him. They are in the drawing room still, next to the radio.

"I'm not going back."

"Oh. But then . . . oh." She realises that it is not her he is going to miss. "Your children were okay with it?" She has talked to them over the radio by now, and she knows how protective his daughters are.

"They were the ones to tell me to go," he says, "You see, they finally looked you up online. I know, I know," he puts up his hands in the air in surrender, "I told you I'd never do such a thing . . ."

"But your daughters were being stubborn?" She laughs.

He nods his head. "After months of seeing me mope around in my house, I guess they grew tired of my sadness. And they wanted to see you the only way they could."

"So if they told you to come to me . . ."

"Yes. They saw your name with mine."

She clutches his hand tightly at his words, reassuring herself that he is real and there with her. She has never felt this happy, and doesn't quite know how to express it.

"They also told me something interesting," he adds. "But I don't know if you'll want to know. Maybe it's best if it stays a surprise for you." He says the last part seriously, but she can catch the grin on his face.

"What is it?"

He doesn't answer at first. He gets up from his seat, and moves towards the front door. There, he turns around and asks her: "If you take the first two letters of your name and join it with the last two of mine. What do you get?"

"IN and KO?"

"Yes. That's right."

"Do you mean . . . ? The library?" Her eyes widen, and she gets up as well. "But wait. Where are you going right now?"

"The book market in Daryaganj," he answers. "It's Sunday, isn't it?"

She still stares at him, processing the weight of his words. She can feel pages turning onto a new chapter. As clichéd as that sounds in her own head.

"Now, come along," Orko says at the precipice. "We have a library to build."

PART II

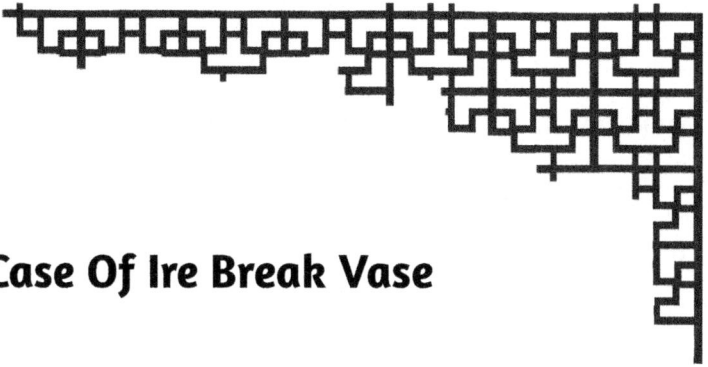

In Case Of Ire Break Vase

7085

It's the first day of August, the beginning of the travel season, and all the houses are shuttered down and folded away. In some cases, entire high-rises have disappeared, leaving behind five-feet wide, two-feet high grey concrete slabs in their wake. Most people have gone off to the past, due to a well-documented phenomenon called "collective nostalgia", which was coined by a 45th century psychologist named Farah Sheikh who wrote the defining book about time travel and how it affects the human mind. She was the one to carefully outline the need, in all of us, to seek history.

"There is a familiarity about the past," Farah had written, "a comfort in knowing the events that will change our lives and that of the others in the years to follow. The future, though within our grasp, though full of adventures and new ideas, is still alien to us. It doesn't have any collective nostalgia to offer—filled as it is with people who will come after us, not with people who made us what we are today.

"That is not to say there aren't those who are so enamoured by the lifestyle hundreds or thousands of years after their own that they spend days, if not months, wandering in the future. Some even take up citizenship, buy a house (or two), and have families in these societies. When they come back, on holidays, to meet their relatives, they behave much like tourists in their old neighbourhoods, asking to be taken on a tour, for the chance to remark 'how things have changed' since they last came here.

"There is a nostalgic element," Farah had written, "in their actions, too."

———◦———

Twenty-three-year-old Samay, who is currently inside his travel pod on an interstate highway between Haryana and Delhi, doesn't fall in either group. He is among the small number of people who truly enjoy being in the present, and is eager to live in the moment. Sure, every year he'll go on a holiday with his mothers—his favourite being when they had gone on a pre-historic safari of New Mexico and had tea next to a sleeping *Apatosaurus*—but it's just another way for him to spend time with them. He never gets a sense of "collective nostalgia", he never wants to stay back and linger. Not like the residents of the grey blocks outside, all folded away. It's a stark sight to behold, but it's inevitable in August, when schools shut down for close to a month, and offices allow for their employees to take time off—all so that they can indulge in a bit of time-hopping.

Samay doesn't go anywhere in August, opting to take a two-week break at the end of the year, to travel with his mothers. He likes the quiet around him—not that it's ever really particularly loud, someone or the other in his housing society is always off in the past or the future. And he likes the 30-minute commute from his office in First Gurgaon, where he works as a design engineer at an architectural firm, to his home in North Campus. He finds peace in watching the empty world pass by—endless fields of wheat on either side of the highway, standing still but for a little wind nudging them every few minutes. But today, things are different. He's upset, annoyed at himself, and everything around him. He can't enjoy the long road down to his home, and wishes for a way to override the system and allow the pea-shaped single-seater to rush past the empty ones dawdling on the highway.

He wishes too, that he could throw out the empty picture frame in his lap. Maybe in the olden days, he might have done that. But now there's an automatic fine for doing so. There's also the fact that if he threw out the frame, he'd lose his flat too. Still, his fingers close over the wooden rectangle and twitch with the desire to fling it out the little window in his travel pod.

He shifts the focus of his glare to the windshield in front of him, where a documentary about conspiracy theorists is being showcased. The self-proclaimed experts, sporting varying lengths of hair, are talking about how they have definite proof that Jantar Mantar, the vast, 18th century sun dial in Connaught Place is responsible for the slow emergence of time travel in Delhi and beyond. According to them, there can only be one reason as to why the phenomenon originated in Delhi and nowhere else. The fact that there are other ancient sun dials in other parts of the country, and the world at large, didn't cause a dent in their reasoning.

"The sun is the source of all life," says a middle-aged man, chewing his words and speaking very slowly, "so it's natural to assume that this boon in our life is a gift from above." He raises his eyes towards the ceiling as he says the last word.

The screen turns black as a hologram of the monument fills up the inside of the pod, appearing as if it's resting on the photo frame. A voiceover informs him that these experts believe a yet-to-be excavated portion of the sun dial is the one "emitting" time molecules, and that though several investigations have shown there's nothing underneath Jantar Mantar, they still think something's lurking below the surface.

"The 'Time Instrument', the 'Samay Yantra'," the voiceover says, which makes Samay's ears perk up, although he knows the narrator is talking about the concept of time, not calling out his name, "lay dormant for thousands of years, before all the planets and stars were finally in alignment and the *time* was right to . . ." Samay switches off the windshield at that moment. He doesn't think he can entertain wild ideas at the moment, not when his own one was so unceremoniously shot down.

———◦———

A couple of months ago, he was at the pod station, on his way to the office, when he'd overheard a child complain to her mother why they had to leave their house behind when travelling to the past. "I want my toys with me," she'd said, her eyes tearing up at the thought. "Why can't we fold our home and carry it with us?"

Her mother had calmly explained to her that it wasn't possible yet, but the moment such a technological feat would become available to them, she'd install it at their house.

That had not only soothed the young girl, and had also planted the seed of an idea in Samay's head. Why *couldn't* they carry a house around? If they could fold the walls, the furniture, and every piece of object inside into a coffin-like structure of cement, surely they could go a step further and fold it into a portable shape that would allow them to never part from their place of residence?

He'd told his boss, Hardeep, the same thing this very morning inside the basement vault, where all new flats were tested. But she had only pursed her lips, tried to give him an encouraging smile, and told him it was not possible.

"What do you mean by that?" he'd asked, watching his very own flat fold into the picture frame, brick by brick.

"I admire the fact that you're thinking out of the box," she'd said instead, "quite literally, in this case." She'd chuckled. "But it's not practical, what you're suggesting. There are so many things that could go wrong."

"Such as?" he'd asked, with disoriented butterflies crashing into each other inside his stomach.

"Very simply, it could get lost—and I know you're thinking of using all kinds of household items as a container for the house . . . ?"

He'd nodded. "Yes," he'd nervously cleared his throat, "socks and key chains, and bottles."

"Things that can easily get lost."

"Well," he'd asked. "What if they were vases or lamps or . . . "

"And what if, due to a little accident, they broke?" Hardeep had asked in return. "Tell me, Samay, do you know why they use concrete slabs to fit the houses and flats in?"

He didn't like her tone. It sounded like she was talking to a child. But he still answered. "Because they are sturdy."

"Exactly. You can kick them, try to move them. But nothing inside will get jostled. Can you do the same with a shoe or *this*?" she wondered, picking up the picture frame from the floor.

"I'll secure the furniture inside, I'll … I'll think of something."

"You're very young, Samay. And I applaud you for going beyond your duties at the firm, and coming up with this idea. The fact that you included your own flat in this shows how dedicated you are," she said, handing him the frame, "but it's just not a practical idea."

He clutches that same picture frame now, as he stands in the hallway, staring at the small rectangular brace he'd drilled into the door a few weeks ago, as a permanent place for the picture frame. All one had to do was gently slide it in, type in a code on the glass, and then wait a few minutes for the insides to unfold and take their place inside his home. He'd done so a hundred times before, without any trouble at all.

But today just isn't his day.

When he tries to fit the picture frame, with perhaps more force than necessary, it gets caught along the edges of the brace and a tiny sliver of wood at the back of the frame gets chipped off. He tries it a second time, inadvertently placing his hand over the chipped off area, which allows a splinter of wood to wedge underneath the skin of his little finger, causing him a shock of pain.

He lets out an "oww" and shakes his hand in the aftermath of the splinter attack. And then he tries again, carefully. There is a clicking sound as the picture frame finally fits into place, followed by four consecutive clicking sounds as he types in the code—his birth year, 7062. And then there's silence, before at once, he hears the "whoosh" of walls falling into place, the "thud" of furniture grounding themselves to the floor, and the "swish" of curtains and bedcovers rushing to their positions. He hears another sound, a sort of crashing, and he realises that Hardeep had been right, that even the tiniest of jostling could disturb the contents of a house.

He doesn't want to go inside and face yet another problem, but he is so very tired at the end of the day, dejected and in need of some rest, and he needs to take out the wooden splinter from his finger lest it gets infected.

So he walks in.

———◆———

Throughout his childhood, growing up near Delhi, in Noida-II, whenever he would run around the house or walk a tad bit faster, his mothers would scold him from whichever part of the house they were in. "If you break the terracotta vase, I'll send you to Old Delhi to replace it," one or both of them would warn him.

"Old" here meant two things: any time period that was so far in the past of their own present that nothing but words like "old" and "ancient" could be used to describe them; any part of Delhi that fell within the boundary of the old Mughal capital city built in the 17th century.

There was also a specific year attached to their threat—1935. According to family lore, it was that very year a certain ancestor on Ankita's side bought the imposing piece of pottery that stared at him from the centre table in his parents' living room. Somehow, in between all the passing-down, it had only suffered one tiny injury, right at its mouth, where a portion of the vase had chipped off.

Unfortunately, its longevity had lent some sort of legend around it—making it into a good luck charm for their family, handed down to each generation and therefore also to Samay when he'd rented this flat. "It'll watch over you," his parents had told him, handing him a vase-shaped bundle on their first visit to his new place. He had no option but to reluctantly accept it and hold in his sigh at their advice to "take good care of it".

Samay has no idea what they would say now, looking upon the destruction in his dining room: the chairs toppled over, the paintings on the walls torn, and the family heirloom—the lovely terracotta vase—in pieces on top of the round dining table.

For a moment, as he stood there, he gave into a panic-induced daydream and imagined turning back time and repairing the vase or, better, stopping himself from breaking it in the first place. But reality returned and he remembered how other people, with far more ambitious plans, had tried to go back in time and correct a course but had found all their ploys implausible in the face of two specific rules of time travel: (1) two versions of an individual couldn't exist in the same moment; and (2) time itself couldn't be reversed to bypass an accident.

Although, to be fair, some people had found a way around the last point—choosing such a path to immortality that it allowed for certain fixes from time to time. So who knew? Perhaps, one day, someone would find a way to repair broken and injured things, as well. But today he has no choice but to travel to 1935, to Old Delhi, to find a repairman who could help him fix the vase.

Before he can do that, though, there are a couple of things he has to take care of: first, there's the splinter in his little finger, for which he goes to the (unharmed) kitchen and places his hand inside the Handcut Glove, resting near his knife-stand. Instantly he feels at peace, as the squishy gel inside the glove envelops his hand, pushes out the wooden stake-like shrapnel, and then heals the wound.

Next, he sends the details of his upcoming trip to a travel agency and, as he waits for them to send him some clothes, he uprights the chairs, fixes the paintings on the wall, and gathers the broken vase in a neat pile on the table.

Fifteen minutes later, a ding goes off in his house as the drawer-elevator in the living room announces an arrival. He walks over to it, opens the sliding door, and finds a thin piece of white cloth, a grey mini-bank (he'd ordered the box variety), two yellow tablets full of universal adapters, a pair of black chappals, a white handkerchief, and a white kurta-pajama set.

As he picks them up, he feels his wallet vibrate in his back pocket—signaling that payment for his purchase had been made. He keeps the clothes on the dining table, for a while, next to the broken vase, while he places the two tablets on his tongue. They dissolve instantaneously, filling his mouth with the language and vocabulary of the time and place he'd be visiting. Not only will the adapters help him speak unknown dialects, but it will also translate conversations to a vocal pattern he is most comfortable with.

There's an odd aftertaste as the universal adapters seep into his tongue, waiting for the moment he'd need to converse in the past, but he's grown used to the peculiar flavour after more than thirty time jumps throughout his life.

Next all there is left to do is wear the clothes and the shoes, and gather all the broken pieces of the vase in the cloth and tie it all up in a bundle. Once he's outside the flat, he types in a code (for the memory chime) on the picture frame, keeping the bundle of vase pressed to his chest, and wonders if he should jump right then and there or go to one of the government-appointed travel zones for the purpose. The transition between times is much smoother there, but there's always a long queue towards it, and he doesn't feel like standing in line, just waiting. So he tells the watch he's ready, and prepares to go through the terms and conditions. In the background, he can hear all the furniture inside his flat moving around, but he focuses his attention on his watch.

There are five lines he has to read and accept before the time machine can transport him:

(1) I, Samay 23Er, will not alter any important, far-reaching events.

(2) I will not kill someone intentionally.

(3) I will not steal wealth or treasures from another time.

(4) Failing to comply with these advisories, I might find myself erased from existence.

(5) I understand all the dangers of time travel, and will not sue the government if something happens to me.

As his eye goes over the last word, the watch clears him for take-off and he goes into his time jump stance—legs slightly apart, face staring straight ahead—but then the door next him opens and his neighbour pokes out his head.

"Oh, good," Dara says, his youthful face smiling at him. "I just caught you in time."

Samay raises his eyebrows in question.

"I heard your flat closing in, you see," Dara adds, pointing his head towards his flat.

"Is there . . . ?" Samay asks.

"Yes, I was wondering if you're going to the 4000s? I needed a certain kind of doorknob. But I see you're going . . . elsewhere?"

"To the 1900s."

"Oh." Dara looks at his clothes more closely. "Are you sure that's right?" he asks.

"Sorry?"

Dara points at Samay's feet. "Are you sure they wore shoes back then?"

"Well, why wouldn't they?"

Dara shrugs. "They were quite primitive back then, weren't they?"

"I . . . don't think so."

"Well, okay. I guess. I'll see you when you come back. Good luck!" he says, and closes the door.

Sometimes Samay wonders why Dara is still here. He doesn't think it out of disrespect. He knows the rest of Dara's family drifted away to other planets a couple of hundred years ago, leaving him behind. But he stayed on, quite content to lead a life here.

Maybe, one of these days, he'll ask Dara in as tactful a manner as possible about this. But for now, he turns his attention back to the watch, straightens into position, and takes off.

1935

He lands in a secluded alley—chosen carefully by the time machine—but doesn't quite place his feet on the ground carefully, and nearly loses his balance. *This is what happens when you jump outside the travel zones,* he laments, as he stretches his right palm in front of him in reflex, trying to not fall over. The vase is still held close to his heart.

An amused giggle reaches him and he freezes in place, eyes downcast. For a second he fears the watch miscalculated and someone saw him jump, but soon he realises he still has his hand out and whoever it is, is chortling at his ridiculous pose. He clears his throat in embarrassment and quickly places his arm by his side.

"I was just," he says, raising his head towards the giggler—a young woman in a dull, off white sari, who is hiding her face with the end of the cloth—standing at the entrance of the alleyway. "I think I . . . lost my balance."

The woman chortles, but still doesn't say anything. So he walks to her, softly, careful with the placement of his feet. He doesn't want to act foolishly in front of her again.

"Namaste," he greets her.

"Namaste," she replies, letting go of her sari and revealing her face to him. She doesn't seem to be much older than him.

"I . . . uh," he begins, and then remembers and opens the bundle under his left arm. "I broke this . . . vase, and I was hoping someone could help me fix it?"

"You need help repairing it?" Her eyes brighten up.

"Yes. Do you know anyone?"

She nods, turning her back on him, motioning him to follow her. "My grandfather, my Dadaji. He has a shop nearby."

It's terribly hot outside, more so since he's grown accustomed to travelling in climate-controlled pods on his streets. And he can already feel sweat gathering along his collar, but still he takes the time to look around, to observe. He glances at the people, dressed like him. (He's relieved to see quite a few of them wearing chappals like his.) And he looks at the buildings and roads, at the tram that slowly moves past them. He nearly bumps into a man with a boxy camera slung over his shoulder as he does so, but quickly recovers with a heartfelt "sorry" before increasing his pace to keep up with his guide.

When finally his eyes take him skywards, he doesn't spy a plane or a hovering car (his parents own one) but he does come across something that stops him in his tracks.

"That's the Ghantaghar," the woman tells him a few seconds later. Upon discovering he was not following her, she had turned around to stand next to him. "Or a 'clocktower' as the British call it. Well, actually, they have a specific name for it, but none of us really use it," she adds quite cheerfully.

"Oh."

"Have you never seen one, wherever you're from?" she asks. "Because I can tell you're not from around here."

"You can?" He looks at her finally.

"You're staring at everything. What else can you be but a tourist?"

He gives a nervous laugh. "I guess . . . Yes, it's quite obvious, isn't it?"

She nods her head. "Now, come along," she says. "If you want to know more about the Ghantaghar and Delhi, Dadaji is the one to ask."

He walks behind her, letting his legs move in auto mode as he thinks about the clocktower he just saw.

For as long as he could remember, people had wondered how time travel first came to be. There were some, like the people in the documentary, who gave in to conspiracy theories. But many wondered if a specific, single person was behind it; or if it was nature itself blessing the world with a new paradigm shift. There had been rumours that a clocktower had a major role to play in it, seeing as their watches acted as time machines for them. But no matter how many times people jumped all over the place and how many clocktowers they had tested, they could not find a source for time travel.

She turns around again, blocking the sun with her hand, waiting for him to catch up. And he lets his thoughts come to a stop.

"It's too hot," he tells her, face to face.

"You're too slow," she answers, grinning, adding, "The shop isn't that far."

She is correct in her assessment, and only five minutes later they are at the doorstep of a two-tiered building. There is an attic at the top, but it looks like nobody lives there. Although it does seem like it might provide a nice vantage point to look at the street below. But that attic is forgotten as he and the woman enter the shop, the ground floor.

It's much cooler inside, and Samay finally feels a bit comfortable in 1935. The smell of varnish and paint relaxes him, too. He glances around, clutching the bundle closer to his chest, while the woman tells him she's going to look for her grandfather.

"He might be in the workshop," she tells him, moving towards a door at the back of the room.

"Sure," he tells her. "I'll wait."

He moves around the space, looking at the shelves and cupboards—catching note of a few beautifully crafted boxes in one of them. He crouches down to take a closer look at them, when a door opens and an amused voice addresses him: "Rekha, quick, get a stick. The monkey's come back."

He turns around in surprise, his mouth forming the words: "No. I was just . . ." But then he sees the woman and an old man beside her, both of them chuckling, and he doesn't complete the sentence.

"Oh! I'm sorry," the man says, as he moves towards Samay. Up close, Samay can see that the man is not much older than 65. His hair is greying, as is his moustache. But his face is still youthful. "But you were crouching down at the exact spot where a monkey had crept into the shop last week. He was also just looking at the boxes." He pauses, looks at his granddaughter, and then adds, "Rekha said you need my help?"

"Yes, with a vase," Samay answers. "It's completely . . ." he trails off as he realises that old man's left arm is much shorter than the other one. He stares at it maybe too long and then gets embarrassed for doing so. "I . . . I apologise . . . I didn't mean to," he says.

But the old man doesn't seem offended at all. "It's human nature to be curious," he says. "And I don't mind. There aren't many in the world like me, with one arm shorter than the other."

"Sorry, I didn't mean to be rude."

"I know," the repairman says, walking up to his grandchild and Samay. "I can see it in your face that you're a bit embarrassed."

"Yes, well, I . . ."

"Dadaji?" the woman, Rekha, steps in. "Can you help him? I have to go and check on Subhash. I was on my way to his house but then I saw *him*," she motions to Samay, before turning her back on them and leaving the two men to their conversation.

"Subhash is my assistant," the man says. "He is recovering from a high fever, so my granddaughter wanted to go visit him. See if he's okay." He pauses in thought, before beginning again. "You might have noticed that she is different. She is much more independent than girls her age."

Samay is not quite sure of the societal norms of the time, so he just nods his head.

"Out of all my children and grandchildren, she is the one who is most like me," he continues. He chortles as he adds: "Everyone thinks the two of us are foolish."

He motions Samay to follow him as he walks towards the counter on the right. "When she turned 14, my son got her married off. It was 'high time', he told me. Although I think he just wanted to take her away from me. He'd once accused me of filling her head with 'nonsense'."

"Is she . . . still married?" Samay asks.

"No. No. He caught tuberculosis, and there was no way out for him. She would have stayed there, at her in-laws, if they had been a bit considerate. But once she became a widow, they started ill-treating her and abusing her. The moment I got to know, I went and brought her back here myself."

He lifts his eyes to Samay's. "I couldn't let her wither there, all alone," he says. "It was a horrible time for her, because of which she is still very wary of people. Although there are some exceptions . . ." He looks up at Samay, watching him curiously.

"I don't know what to . . . say."

The old man chuckles. "Now, show me, where is this vase of yours?"

Samay places the broken vase, still bundled up, on the wooden counter between them, and opens up the ties. "This has been in our family for a long time, and today, well, I accidentally broke it . . . Will you be able to fix it?"

"Are you sure all the pieces are here?" he says.

"Yes, I think so."

"Hmm. You know what would be a better idea?" the repairman says, moving out from behind the counter and catching Samay by the elbow and moving him towards the main door. "There's a potter right around the corner. I know him very well—his name is Vivek. Go to him, he might have a vase that looks exactly like yours. He might even build you a replica if he's in a good mood."

They are outside now, on the streets of Chandni Chowk,

and Samay can see earthen pots and vases close by. He turns to look at the old man next to him and opens his mouth to say thanks. But instead he says, "I'll be back in a few minutes. Can I leave the broken vase with you?"

"Of course."

Samay thanks him and moves ahead. He rifles through the mini-bank in his pocket and presses a button to print out some rupees, preparing to buy a new terracotta vase. When he returns to the shop, he keeps the vase (luckily he'd found an identical one) on the counter and thanks the repairman for his help.

"No problem," he says, watching Samay tie up the broken one in a bundle. "I'm Arun, by the way."

"And I'm Samay."

"Are you?" He guffaws. "There's a monument dedicated to you a few streets away. Did you see it?"

"Oh . . . the clocktower? Yes. I saw that on my way here. Have you . . ." he says as casually as possible, "have you seen anything odd happening around that place?"

"Odd? Like what?"

"I don't know. I just . . . haven't seen anything like that before."

For a moment Samay worries Arun will ask him where he's from. But instead the old repairman says, "You know, I'm a bit envious of the Ghantaghar."

"You . . . what?" Samay is caught off guard, to say the least. "I don't understand."

"You probably think I'm being foolish." Arun looks a bit embarrassed. He's stopped working on the dollhouse for the moment, and is leaning his palms on the table.

"No," Samay tries to cover up. "I'm sure you have a reason for it."

"I'm afraid even the reason is a bit foolish." He laughs.

"I'm getting old," Arun says, subconsciously adjusting his glasses. "My eyesight isn't the same. Even my bones are getting tired. I don't know what will happen to my granddaughter after I'm gone. I don't know what will happen to my shop. None of my children want it. Maybe, I'll give it away to Subhash, that's a possibility."

He pauses.

"Although I have a house, in Daryaganj, this shop is my home," he continues. "This is where I belong. This job is what I was meant to do, it was written in my destiny. But . . . I wish there was a way for me to stay here, forever. To help people and solve their problems. I wish I was that clocktower outside. Eternal. Watching over people, keeping them on time. Always in the same place. Dependable and resolute."

He sighs.

"But none of that is possible."

7085

Months go by, and Samay settles back into his life. He goes to work, he comes home, sometimes he meets Dara in the hallway or when either of them is locking or unlocking their flats. One day, when he arrives at his front door, a welcome sight is awaiting him.

"What are you two doing here?" he asks with a smile.

His mothers both laugh. "We thought we'd pay you a surprise visit," Ankita says. She is the shorter of the two, with curly hair.

"I hope you aren't busy," Zoya adds. She is the worrier, always wondering if she isn't inconveniencing anyone.

"No, of course not," Samay answers. He types in the code on the picture frame, which is now filled with a photo of him and his mothers from their prehistoric trip, and ushers them in.

"I love that photo of ours," Zoya says. "What made you put it up on the door?"

"It was just some project that didn't take off," he replies sheepishly.

"For work?" Ankita asks, just to be sure.

"Yes," he sighs. "It was a half-baked idea, to be honest," he adds, sitting down on the sofa with his parents, as the walls of the living room turn a mix of light green and purple. He'd engineered the walls to reflect his mothers' favourite colours when they were in any room.

"I'm sure you gave it your 100%," Zoya says, patting his knee. She's sitting right next to him on the sofa while Ankita is on the floating sofa chair on their left.

"I think so," he answers.

"We know so," they answer in unison.

He chuckles. "So, how have the two of you been?"

"We're fine, we're the same as we ever were," Ankita says, waving a hand dismissively. "We want to know about you. Any . . . exciting developments?"

"Do you want some tea or coffee?" he asks instead, hovering his hand above the centre table.

"Black coffee."

"Lemon tea."

He presses the button at the centre of the table and clearly enunciates what his parents want. A second later, two circular openings appear on the surface, through which two cups appear. One is filled with coffee and the other with tea. Samay hands them both their preferred beverage, opting to drink nothing himself.

"Exciting developments? Hmm," he says, as he sits down again. "Well, I went to 1935 a few months ago."

"The year?" Ankita asks.

Zoya turns to look at her, her cup not yet at her lips. "Well, what else can it be?"

"I don't know what young people are into these days." Ankita shrugs.

Zoya shakes her head at her, smiling. "So," she looks at Samay, "you went to 1935. Did you meet anyone there? Anyone famous?" She had a diary where she noted down all the historical figures they had interacted with. She was currently at page 32.

"No. Nobody famous. I *did* meet some interesting locals. A repairman called Arun and his granddaughter, Rekha. She must have been around my age. She was so strange . . . but in a good way." He smiles.

"Was she?" Zoya asks, exchanging a look with Ankita.

"Ye-es. I mean, for her time . . . she was unusual. She wouldn't seem out of place here."

"Of course, she wouldn't," Ankita guffaws.

He blushes but doesn't rise to the bait. And Zoya gently prods him for more information.

"So what did you talk about?"

"She was out visiting someone, so while I waited for her, I talked to her grandfather about clocktowers and the meaning of time. He took me to his workshop and showed me a dollhouse he was repairing, and I helped him a bit with it. I told him I built things too, so I knew a few things."

"And with Rekha?" Zoya asks.

"Not much. I . . . I don't really remember."

"Hmm," Ankita says. "Wait, you didn't tell us why you travelled to 1935 in the first place. Were you looking for something specifically?"

"Yes, the thing is . . ." he says, and stops with growing realisation. He looks towards the dining table, the very empty dining table, and his eyes widen in alarm.

Ankita notices his gaze towards the dining table, and registers the absence as well. She turns her head towards him, questioning, "Didn't you keep the vase over there?"

1935

"What did you break this time?" Rekha says the moment he enters the repair shop. She and her grandfather had been sitting behind the counter, talking amongst themselves, when he'd walked in.

Samay chortles a little. "No, I didn't break anything, but I think I might have . . ."

"Forgotten the vase over here?" Arun finishes for him. "I

realised you'd left it on the counter that very night, when we were closing up."

"We kept it for a few days," Rekha adds, "hoping that you'd come back and take it. But then when it turned into months . . . Subhash took it home."

"Subhash?" Samay asks.

"My assistant. He's in the workshop, cleaning up. I'll call him here . . . Subhash!" He shouts the last bit.

"He really liked the vase," Rekha says. "Said he wanted to gift it to his mother, and we . . . gave it to him."

"We'll pay you the amount, of course," Arun whispers as Subhash enters the room. He is a boy of about 14, gangly and a bit timid. "I don't want to cut any money from his salary," Arun adds, still whispering.

Samay feels unsettled with how young the boy is, but he reminds himself that he's thousands of years in the past. And that their society is much different from his.

"Namaste, Subhash," he tells the boy, who folds his hands at him and then goes back to the workshop.

Samay turns to Arun and tells him there's no need. He'll buy the vase again, he doesn't mind. But Arun insists. And Arun again tells him that it's alright, he'll pay for the vase, but again Arun reiterates that he'd like to pay for the inconvenience. This goes on for a minute or two before Rekha steps in.

"Why don't you give me the money, Dadaji, and I'll go with Samay and ensure he buys the vase with it?"

Samay means to protest again, but she shushes him, grabs hold of his hand and takes him outside.

"Don't worry," she tells him, once they're on their way to

the potter. "I'll let you buy the vase. I just couldn't stand the two of you talking in circles." She giggles.

He grins. "Are you always at the shop?" he wonders.

"Yes. I really enjoy helping Dadaji with the customers, and even with the repair work. Subhash is still learning, so I try to help the two of them as much as I can."

"You're very lucky to have such a grandfather," he says. And he means it.

"I know," she simply says, and then softly asks, "Are you going to visit us again?

"I don't know."

There is nothing to bring me back here, he thinks. But then she beams at him, bright and wonderful. Hopeful. And he says, "Maybe. I think I might."

———◦———

The years between 7085 and 7100

He weds Rekha only a few years later (in her time, since the concept of marriage was dissolved sometime in the 57th century), and they tossed a coin (from her time, again) to decide where they would live. It spun for a long time on the shop counter before landing on tails (his time, not hers).

Arun and Rekha, and even Subhash to some degree, had known for some time that Samay was not from their world. Samay had already taken Arun and Rekha thousands of years into their future a couple of times—holding hands to make sure they didn't fall off the time-tunnel—and shown them around the place; let them meet the people in his life: his mothers, his travel agent, and his neighbour, Dara, who struck up an easy friendship with Arun. But after the wedding, their travels became a weekly pilgrimage.

Back and forth the three of them would come and go, into the future and then to the past—more so after Samay bought Arun and Rekha their own time machines—but no matter how many times Samay and Rekha asked Arun to stay on with them, he always wanted to go back home. "I don't want to leave the shop in Subhash's hands. God knows what he'll do to the place if I stay away for a long time," he'd say.

Samay's life had progressed on another front as well: he had upgraded the idea that his boss had thought so impractical a few years ago, changing it after Arun had remarked that there weren't many entertainment avenues in Samay's time. That there weren't that many buildings, either.

It was true, his was a very minimalistic world. Not only were single units the preferred choice of lifestyle, with a few like his mothers opting for a family unit of two or three, even the flats and houses they all lived in were capable of folding themselves into small boxes and allow wider open spaces for people to move around in. Their interior decoration was much the same, with only the basic necessities and furniture required for a seamless life finding space in houses and flats. Often, the only piece of decorative items were family heirlooms that had been passed down generations for hundreds and thousands of years.

Some said their modest lifestyle was part of a larger societal change. That after the three millennia-long age of maximalism—overcrowded with cities and information (in lieu of a chip that was later discontinued after a virus fried a million brains), and polyamorous relationships—there was bound to be a period such as theirs. But Samay and many others believed there were several more factors, that the truth was that there just weren't as many people on Earth anymore. The birth rate was down, it had been for a long time; and those that chose the path of immortality (like Dara) and opted to transfer their consciousness to a synthetic body frame, often moved to faraway planets, way beyond Mars and the Moon. They didn't need the life support system the two outlier civilisations were founded on; but more than that, those that still stayed on spent so much of their time travelling to the past or the future—and stayed there for so long—that even the most popular of cities only ever had a few thousand citizens living inside it at any given moment of time.

That was the reason their houses were engineered to fold away into compact forms when their residents were away. It was a safety measure, to ensure no one could break in and steal something. It also meant no dust could gather inside. An added feature was the memory chime, which came into force whenever a potential thief would step inside the vicinity of a folded house. A bell would ring, cause a temporary memory lapse, and confuse the person into leaving the premises.

When Samay had come up with his picture frame idea, his thought had been to take this feature to the next step—to help people carry their homes with them. But as his boss, Hardeep, had pointed out, it wasn't very foolproof.

For years, then, he had shelved the idea.

It was only after Arun commented about the absence of entertainment that Samay realised he should look at his idea from another angle. He realised he could very well modify the houses: into roller coasters and interactive statues, into arcades where people could play games the ancient way—the possibilities were endless. His boss thought so too, and approved the concept even before Samay had time to build a prototype.

When he did build one, he took inspiration from the man who had started it all. He used Arun's shop as the default structure and constructed a grandfather clock on its flip side, with its features emulating that of the Ghantaghar in Chandni Chowk. Soon enough, his creations began to fill the landscape around him. And people, the ones who remained, began to flock to them. Others, his competitors, started constructing similar buildings, and the world became a brighter, more enjoyable place to live in.

1950

Samay has a bit of grey in his hair now, despite only being in his early 40s. There is a beard covering half his face, and his pair of white pajamas and kurta are so well worn that there are creases all over them. This time when he lands, his feet hit the ground with a gentle thud and he immediately moves out of the secluded alley onto the main road.

Out in the open, he takes some time to look around the changed city. A few years into independence, there is an air of hope and resilience everywhere—sticking to the walls like fresh paint. As he breathes it in, he catches a whiff of something most delicious and slows down to let his nose take him on a little detour.

There, a few stores to his left, a new mithai shop is gathering tourists and locals alike to its doors. And right there, in a massive vessel, swirls of jalebis are being fried in a swift and delicate manner. He's had a few with Arun and Rekha before, and he knows how much they both love the syrupy, crunchy sweet, so he stands in front of the shop and waits for the jalebis to cook to a crisp.

He is just about to buy some for his family when a loud rumble reverberates throughout the place. Even the ground shakes a bit. He turns around, brows tied up in confusion, and is further mystified when he starts to hear shouts and screams from the road ahead. The jalebis are now forgotten as he joins a crowd of curious passersby to see what could have caused the commotion.

Samay has never seen a building collapse before, he has only ever seen them fold and unfold. So when he moves forward and sees the Ghantaghar broken and in pieces, its bricks sticking out, people gathered around it and panicking, it takes some time for him to understand what has happened. He moves with the crowd, towards the collapsed structure. He cannot interfere, but with professional curiosity in his mind, he moves slowly to see the scene from every angle.

It is only when he sees a man injured, bleeding from the head, and when he recognises the man to be Arun that he rushes to his old friend. Others around Samay recognise him to be Arun's grandson-in-law, and they make way for him.

"Arun?" he asks, voice shaking. The man himself is sitting on the ground, legs open, looking dazed and concussed. His eyes are still open but Samay doesn't know how long they'll stay open. He knows he has to take Arun with him, to a hospital in his time, to ensure everything is alright. But he knows he'll need some help. "Subhash?" He looks around, but can't see him anywhere.

He sees a mix of faces around him—some concerned, others fascinated by tragedy—but he doesn't see Subhash. And then he does. He has a few scratches on his face, but he seems to be unhurt otherwise. He staggers out of the crowd and moves to sit next to Samay and Arun.

"I was," he says, "I was just . . . looking for a telephone, to call an ambulance, but now . . ."

"I'm here," Samay says, propping up Arun to stand. "I need to take him . . . Can you help me?"

Together, even as people keep chattering around them, and more keep coming to see what is happening, Samay and Subhash carry Arun over to his shop.

"I'll take him to a hospital there, don't worry," Samay tells Subhash, who has tears in his eyes by now. "You're okay, aren't you?"

Subhash nods.

"Was anybody else hurt?"

"I think . . . I'm not sure. It just happened so quickly. We were walking past the Ghantaghar and then it just . . . there was a loud noise and there were bricks everywhere."

Once inside the shop, which they make sure to lock from the inside, they head to the workshop. Together, they keep Arun upright as Samay presses the emergency button on his watch, which takes them directly to a hospital in his time.

7100

"How are you feeling?" Samay asks as he sees Arun open his eyes for the first time in a couple of hours.

Arun, who is still under the effects of the healing sleep, feels a bit drowsy. His eyebrows draw up in a quizzical formation as he opens his mouth to ask a question. "Wha . . . happen . . . ?"

"You had a little accident, but you're fine now."

"Subh . . . sh?"

"He's fine, too. He's taking care of the shop now."

"Oh. Rek . . . ?"

"She'll be here in a few minutes. She's gone to talk to the doctor." Rekha had been distraught at seeing her grandfather injured, and had been constantly worrying that his old age would make his injuries slow to heal. She'd been told several times that there was nothing to worry about, but she couldn't help but do exactly that.

"Oh. I . . . goo . . ." Arun blinks a couple of times, gaining a better handle on his consciousness.

"I dreamt," he says.

"Yes? And what did you see?"

"I . . . was walking past the Ghantaghar . . . and then it . . . fell on me and . . . killed me. But then . . . it picked me up?"

"It did?"

"Ye . . . and then suddenly . . . I was the clock. My arms . . . were the hands? Hour," he says, lifting his shorter arm and then letting it fall with a thud on his bed. "Minute," he says, doing the same with his other arm. "And I was . . . helping people." His eyes widen with conviction at that statement.

"You were?"

Arun softly nods. "My shop . . . it was there too." He suddenly looks beseechingly at Samay. "Will you help me? Build it? I know . . . you can."

It was only a dream. And many who have been sleep-healed get fantastical ideas in their heads after waking up from it. It's taken as a good sign, proof of the fact that the brain is functioning well. Yet, Samay can't help but wonder if some of it could be turned into a reality.

He broaches the topic with Rekha first, to gauge if what he is thinking is a good idea or not. But she doesn't even want to look beyond the first point.

"You want to turn my Dadaji into a robot?" she shouts at him, at their flat.

"We don't use that word anymore, Rekha."

"Sorry." She shakes her head. "I just don't want him to . . . change and become someone else."

"But he won't. Everyone retains their memories, you know that."

"Only if they choose to."

"What?"

"Dara told me, how most people choose to suppress memories of their past life and start anew, in another world. A fresh start. His own family did that. He said there *is* a change that comes over them after the transfer. That it can't be helped, and that it's sourced from the synthetic setup."

"Then why is *he* still here?"

"You go ask him that. But I'm not going to let my grandfather be turned into a little project for you. I've seen you moping around, Samay. I know you're itching to get your hands on another . . . outlandish concept, that'll make people celebrate you again."

"That's not true," he feebly states.

She glares at him and folds her arms.

"But," he tries, "you've said so yourself, that he's growing older and you wish for him to come stay with us, so that we can take care of him. If he were to get a synthetic frame, you would never have to worry about him. He'll have a self-repairing system in place!"

Unfortunately, his words don't have the desired effect on her and she visibly flinches at the last line.

"He'll be a machine." Her voice quivers.

"In a sense."

"And he'll forget me and you, and everyone."

He sighs. "No, he won't."

"Can you prove that?"

"I can't prove anything without . . ."

"Then I can't allow this to happen."

"But Rekha . . ." he says, as she turns around and leaves the house. If he knows her well, she'll take one of those movie pods and travel around Noida for the duration of a film of her choice. She says the motion of the pod soothes her and the sounds from the screen help distract her when she is troubled or anxious.

He gives her the time to take the lift and go to the pod station, before opening the front door himself. Once he's outside the flat, he types in the code for the memory chime, wondering who could help him with this problem.

In the background, he can hear all the furniture inside his flat moving around, as the door next him opens and his neighbour pokes out his head.

"Oh, good," Dara says, his youthful face smiling at him. "I just caught you in time."

Samay raises his eyebrows in question.

"I heard your flat closing in, you see," Dara adds, pointing his head towards his flat.

"Is there . . . ?" Samay asks.

"Yes, I was wondering if Arun is okay? I heard he got into an accident."

"He did, yes. And he's fine now. But Rekha . . ."

"Is worried, I know. We've been talking."

Samay narrows his eyes at him. "I know. She told me."

"What's the issue here?" Dara closes the door behind him and stands in the hallway with Samay.

"You told her that your family left Earth."

"Which is true. And she asked me, so I told her."

"You also told her that they chose to delete their memories, and start fresh."

"Also true. What exactly is the problem here, Samay?"

He breathes out and calms himself, tries to rein himself in. "I proposed that we offer Arun a chance at the same process. He's already 80, and I don't know if the medical centres in his time are capable of taking care of him. But she is adamant that he'll forget her and . . ."

"Leave her?" Dara finishes. "Yes, she has a point."

"You're not helping."

Dara smiles. "She has the right to know, Samay. But, maybe I could tell her why my Lifegiver chose the process, and why I stayed behind?"

"You would?" Samay had thought it was too personal a question to ask.

"Sure," Dara pats him on the shoulder. "Anything to help you, Samay."

"Oh. I just . . . is it okay, if . . . can I ask? Why *didn't* you leave with them?"

"Because this place, this world, is my home. This is where my Lifegiver was born. This is where he weathered his miseries and celebrated his joys. This is where he eventually elected to pass on and transfer his consciousness to a synthetic frame of his likeness—to me. Why would I want to be anywhere else?"

"That . . . that makes sense," Samay says, turning around to go back into his flat. But then Dara says something that makes Samay look back at him in confusion.

"You know," he says, "you could just go to Chandni Chowk right now and check for yourself."

"What do you mean?" Samay wonders.

"Chandni Chowk would be inside Analog District, right?" Dara asks.

Samay slowly nods.

"So there would be an information kiosk in front of every establishment, which would show when it was built, what purpose it served, and everyone who came to own the building over time. You could just read about what happened to Arun standing in front of his shop," Dara explains.

"But that is *if* Arun's shop is still there," Samay answers. "It might have been destroyed thousands of years ago."

"Yes," Dara says. "That is a possibility. But how will you know for sure unless you see for yourself?"

———◦———

The pod drops him off just outside Analog District, the one place in Delhi where folding buildings aren't allowed—where things maintain a distinct old world charm (i.e., belonging to a time before the 55th century). Samay walks close to half an hour to reach what used to be called Chandni Chowk and a few minutes more to stand in front of Arun's old shop. He is pleasantly surprised to see it still standing, more so since it doesn't seem to have aged one bit from the 1950s. And yet, he frowns, for he cannot see any information kiosk nearby. Every store on the road has one, barring this one.

Maybe I should talk to the proprietor and see what they have to say? he thinks and takes a step inside the repair shop.

The moment he does so, a feeling of deep knowing climbs up his limbs and lights a spark in his mind. He can see the overwhelmed cupboards in his periphery, the shelves floating above him—carrying weights of mobile phones and telephones of yore—but his eyes can't budge from the teak door that leads to the workshop. His heart speeds up in anticipation, as he places his hand on the handle and twists it downward.

He stops with the door still ajar and looks on at the scene in front of him: Arun is focused on repairing the shop's prototype (aged and worn in his hands)—the one Samay had only recently given him, in 1949—sitting on top of a table.

"Hello, Samay," Arun greets him without preamble. When he receives no answer, he looks up at him for a second. "Are you really *that* surprised to see me?"

"I . . . uh . . . didn't expect . . ."

"But isn't this the proof you wanted? Well, the proof that Rekha wanted . . ."

"It is, but . . . I just didn't . . ." Samay repeats himself.

". . . expect it?" Arun leaves the prototype for the moment and grins. "Yes, I got the feeling that you didn't."

"It's just . . . shock." Samay finally closes the wooden door behind him and walks towards Arun.

"It's one thing to say something, to think of it even, and quite another to see it manifested . . . is it not?" Arun asks.

Samay nods. He feels absurd asking this question, but he needs to be sure. "You're not . . . alive, are you? That is to say . . ."

"No. Not in the biological sense. The man you've known all these years is still in hospital, recuperating. He is my Lifegiver. I'm the next step in his evolution—the result of the fever dream he told you."

"But then . . . why are you here? *How* are you here? I know for certain that the Arun I know—your Lifegiver—is still healing and hasn't been synthesised . . . yet."

The synthetic Arun leans against the table and tells him how, in a few months' time, his Lifegiver will breathe his last, come alive as a fully functioning synthetic ("Who is standing before you right now," he adds) and elect to go back to the 1950s. Rekha will want her newly-furbished Dadaji to stay back, but he will argue that he has a responsibility to help people, especially those who don't have access to 72nd century technology.

"I will . . ." Arun says, and then corrects himself. "I *have* spent thousands of years repairing all sorts of things for all sorts of people. I've seen cities change like seasons. I've seen millions die and millions taking birth. But still I've waited here, for this moment, for you to walk in through the doors and have this very conversation with me."

"You knew I was coming here today?"

"I did!" Arun cheerfully informs him. "Today's a pretty important day, you'll see."

"But the fact that you *both* are here . . . that doesn't break any time rule?" Samay asks. "I thought two versions of the same individual couldn't exist in the same timeframe?"

"Ah, but you see." Arun grins. "Despite having the same behaviour patterns and the same personalities, we are two entirely different people who exist in entirely different bodies. I have my Lifegiver's memory files, yes, but he doesn't have mine."

"O-kay," Samay says slowly. "So this loophole . . . it must exist for all synthetics?"

"It does. But most of them leave this world, do they not? And those who stay, how many of them travel?"

"I haven't heard of anyone."

"Because they don't."

"It's that simple?"

"*Some* things are."

"And what are the complicated things?" Samay asks. He's intrigued by the wording of Arun's sentence.

"Well, my core processor for one. That's not an easy component to make. It's quite unique, you see."

"What do you mean?"

Arun changes course. "I think you should pay me a visit."

"But, then . . ."

"In the past. Pay me a visit in the past, and see for yourself."

"You won't tell me now?" Samay asks.

Arun shakes his head. "No, you have to *see* it."

Samay sighs. "At least tell me *when* I should go?"

"*That* I will tell you."

Third Time's The Charm

1986

Arun told him to meet him any time in the late 20th century or the early 21st century. But failed to tell him the exact time. Samay takes a guess and lands in the afternoon, during lunch hour. He hopes the shop is empty, that there are no customers inside. But just as he catches sight of the shop from a distance, he sees an old man and two young children enter the building with a heavy suitcase in tow.

He waits outside for a while, hoping that their business will be concluded soon, but when it seems like Arun and the old man have started a conversation among themselves, and they are quite comfortable in exchanging memories, Samay leaves and looks elsewhere.

1994

It's evening, and he hopes people are on their way back home, and that no one is really interested in a quaint repair shop. Samay walks with purpose, taking in the changed environs—the

unhealthy amount of cars and people on the road—and is glad
that he'd taken the anti-pollution vaccine as a child.

Up ahead he sees a man carrying a TV set in his arms, and
struggling to do so. He offers to help him, and is later quite
disheartened to see where he is going—right into Arun's shop.
As he holds the door open for the man, who utters no word of
thanks, he catches sight of a woman inside the shop, behind the
counter. Her face looks awfully familiar, but he can't recognise
her.

Arun is nowhere to be seen, though. And he tries his luck a
third time.

2016

It's early morning, when Chandni Chowk is still drowsy, and the
streets are empty. Samay doesn't think he'll face any problems
today, but he can't be sure, so he quickens his pace the moment
he appears in a secluded alley.

He's been to the shop so many times before that he doesn't
even think, he just lets his feet make the decisions—over well-
traced paths—and deposit him in front of Arun's repair shop.
For ten minutes he roams around, overjoyed to experience the
peace and quiet in such a usually crowded marketplace. For the
first time he can actually hear the pigeons flapping their wings,
flying past him, probably on their way to Jama Masjid, the 17th
century mosque that was nearby, for some sprinklings of seeds.
And he can see people carrying bags of cardamom, cinnamon,

and cloves—filling the air with potent scents—to the nearby spice market of Khari Baoli.

But as he nears the shop, he begins to feel that something is amiss. From where he's standing, right across the road, Arun's shop would be straight ahead. But instead in front of him is a clocktower, the very same one that had fallen on Arun and sent him to the hospital.

As he stands there, confused, a woman appears and draws shapes on the clocktower—on three specific bricks. (There are only four others on the street other than them, but they are all more occupied with opening their stores.) In a few seconds, Samay hears a deep rumble from within the structure, and then the whole building begins to move—the clock dives inside, the bricks fall apart and move into place, and paint starts to appear on newly-formed walls.

"Oh," is all Samay says, coming to a realisation.

The woman looks around, focusing on the early-risers, who are staring up at the building, and waits a few seconds.

"Ding" comes the sound of the memory chime, and the four strangers shake their heads, forgetting what they had just witnessed, and go back to their work. But Samay still stares at the building, which has now transformed to Arun's shop. He looks at every little detail before resting his eyes on the woman, who is shocked beyond belief to see him unfazed.

He waves at her, but still she doesn't move. It's only when he crosses the road and moves towards her that she bolts for the door of the shop. She is about to lock it from the inside when a familiar voice calls out and asks her to stop.

"I know him, Jaya," Arun says, as he gently pushes the

woman aside. "Hello, Samay," he says, as he opens the door for him.

As he enters, he attempts a second wave at Jaya but she still seems wary of him.

"I'd told her that everyone, without fail, would get hypnotised by the chime . . . and then you showed up," Arun tells him.

"He's the one who built this place anew," Arun tells Jaya, gesturing toward the visitor. "He's the one who installed the chime in the first place."

Jaya widens her eyes and looks at him. "Oh, I didn't know."

"Sorry about earlier," Samay says. "I didn't mean to scare you."

"That's alright," she answers, moving behind the counter. Arun is still standing next to the door with Samay.

"Can I ask you something?" Samay wonders. Jaya nods.

"Your face seems very familiar to me," he asks. "Have we met before?"

"No. But you might have met my grandfather, Subhash?"

"How astonishing," he says. "I mean, of course, you can follow your grandfather's footsteps, but still . . ."

"Oh wait," Jaya says. "Are you the one who gave us the terracotta vase?"

"That's right, I am." He pauses. "Is it still okay? Do you still have it?"

She laughs, embarrassed. "I still have it, yes. But this very morning there was a little accident, and I chipped off a tiny portion of it at the mouth. Sorry about that."

"It's not a coincidence, is it?" Samay asks later, when Arun and he are inside the workshop. Jaya is cleaning up the counter and the shelves, readying the shop for customers.

"No," Arun replies. "It's not."

"The day I came here, all those years ago . . ."

"You were just closing a loop . . . or starting one."

"This is just . . . incredible," Samay says. And then he stares at Arun. "Is that why you sent me here, to meet Jaya?"

"I can't say for sure. You'll have to ask *him*, the 'me' that sent you here."

Samay tries another line of questioning. "When did you know? That Jaya is my great-great-great—whatever number it is—grandmother?"

Arun laughs. "I've known for a long time. That was one of the first things you told Lifegiver at the hospital."

"I . . . uh. I don't . . ." Samay sighs and sits down on a lopsided stool near the table and hangs his head in his palms. He feels overwhelmed, unsure of what to do.

"There, there," Arun comforts, patting his head. "You'll get the hang of it."

"You . . . you don't find any of this unusual?" Samay asks, looking up at him.

"When you get to my age, you get used to things like this," Arun says.

"And what about Jaya? Is she okay with this . . . setup? Are you keeping her here because she's Subhash's granddaughter, or does she own the shop . . ."

"Oh, no. No. Nothing like that. It's true that her ancestry is important, that because she has been to this shop since her childhood, I can trust her and rest easy that she will never reveal my secret."

Samay opens his mouth to ask, but Arun is one step ahead of him. "This world wouldn't accept a synthetic amongst them. If they knew who I was, they would capture me, make me live in a zoo, or worse, tear me apart and look inside me. Jaya is a barrier, she protects me, and ensures that the shop is safe. You saw for yourself how careful she was opening it."

Samay nods. And then gets up as he remembers something. "You told me a few hours ago, in the year—"

"7100?"

"Yes. But how did you know?" Samay says, surprised once again by the Aruns' depth of knowledge.

"I have a sharp memory." Arun taps the centre of his chest. "Now, what were you saying?"

"I was going to ask you a question about that." He points right to where Arun had touched. "Your core processor. The other 'you' said it was special."

"It is!" His eyes brighten up. "Do you want to see it?" he asks, but doesn't wait for an answer, and instantly takes off his kurta to allow a portion of his chest to open outward, like a door. Inside is a chrome-plated maze of gears and compartments, wired up in colours of red, green and blue. The entire setup is bathed in warm yellow light, to allow every part of Arun's inner mechanics to be visible even in the dark.

In other synthetics, such as Dara, the core processor was the same as the ones inside the travel pods and the folding houses—a simple but powerful CoreP25 disk that allowed the intellect, the language portal, the limbs, and other compartments to function at their best capacity. But in Arun's case . . .

"Is that a time machine?" Samay says, in awe.

"Yes. And the same kind you're wearing on your wrist. This one isn't registered in the government records, though," Arun replies. "So they can't track me. That was your idea, by the way. At least, that's what you told my Lifegiver. But now," he looks at Samay curiously, "I'm not so sure. Maybe you got the idea from me?"

Samay doesn't say anything, but looks more closely inside Arun. At the centre, encased in a golden wire mesh, is a watch much like the one Samay is wearing on his left wrist. The dial is facing him, glowing and buzzing. The numbers are displayed up to the seventh place, and are constantly changing following a seemingly random pattern. The straps, the darkest of blues, are keeping the watch tied into the system, wrapped around as they are to the cylinder that holds the coolant.

"How does that affect you?" Samay asks finally, meeting Arun's eyes. "How do you use it to help people?"

The old man promptly closes his skin, wears his kurta again, and points towards the gramophone player that has been waiting on the table next to them. "Why don't you try this?" he says.

A record is already in place, Samay only has to place the tone arm for the music to start playing through its wide, flower-like horn. It's the oddest kind of music: a soft, soothing lullaby with hints of underlying sadness. He feels drowsy and closes his eyes, and then he's a baby again, inside the Child Rearing Facility where he was born. His mothers are looking down on him, their faces streaked with happiness. Ankita reaches a shaky finger towards him, briefly touching his button nose, and he comes back to Arun's workshop.

"What was that?" he asks. He feels a bit intimidated by the older man, a bit scared even.

"Don't worry, Samay," Arun replies, landing a hand on his shoulder. "It was just a memory from your first day."

"How did the gramophone access it?" He feels a bit annoyed. "Did you hack into my files and . . ."

"No. No. Nothing like that. I don't even know what you saw. I only know that the gramophone allows for the listener to relive their childhood."

"Did you make this?" Samay asks, relieved.

"I repaired it. I used the balm of time," he places a hand on his own chest, "and healed it. I made it the way it is now. So, yes, I guess," Arun shrugs, "I made this."

"The 'balm of time'?" Samay raises his eyebrows. "What does that mean? What are the mechanics behind it?"

"You'll know soon enough. At the right moment."

"I wish the two of you wouldn't do that," Samay says, slightly annoyed. "I wish you wouldn't just . . . postpone telling me the truth."

"Sorry," Arun says. "But . . . I could tell you something else? I could tell you how I knew for certain how to fix the gramophone . . . how to fix anything that comes my way, really."

Samay doesn't say anything, but Arun can see he is intrigued. He continues, "See, the watch inside not only heals, but it also helps me understand *what* the customer wants—it gives me an essence of what they're missing in life. Now, the owner of the gramophone kept talking about how her father used to play songs on the gramophone when she was a child. And that she envies the person she used to be—carefree and happy. I . . . wanted her to feel that way, actually *feel* it, when using this gramophone."

"Did you know just by looking at her what she wanted, or did your conversation with her help you understand what needed to be done?" Samay asks.

"Both," Arun responds. "Actually, if you want to know more about her, you should talk to Jaya. She was the one at the counter while I was in here, working on a cassette recorder. Let me call her in here. Just wait a second, will you?"

So saying, he moves towards the door. "Jaya? Are you there?" he enquires with his hand on the handle.

When it opens, Arun stops in his tracks and says, "Sorry, I'll be with you soon. I didn't realise a customer was here." He turns around to face Samay then, who has been standing right behind him, and tells him that they'll talk later.

"I can see that you still have a lot of questions," he continues, "but you'll have to ask me some other time. I'm needed here." He nods towards the customer, a middle-aged woman, as he says that. She has a radio in front of her, on the counter.

Samay still hesitates. "But . . . will you be okay? Do you need my help in any way?"

"No, Samay." He beams at him. "All I've ever wanted was to help people, to be an eternal repairman, and thanks to you I've achieved that."

As Samay parts, he takes one look at Jaya and waves at her. He wonders if she knows the connection between them, that he is her descendant. He never got the chance to ask her; he was too shocked to say anything after the chipping comment, and Arun had dragged him inside to show him the gramophone.

His thoughts are still in disarray, slowing folding into the form of comprehension. And so, it is only when he's returned to his time, when he's on his way to an older Arun, that everything falls into place in his mind.

EPILOGUE

Sunlight is dimming outside, no lights have been switched on inside the shop. Still, the man from before, now older and wearier, has no trouble navigating the shadowy space. His path is straight, to the door at the back of the shop. He opens it with purpose and is momentarily blinded by the bright spotlights within. An older man, in his 80s, is applying a fresh coat of varnish to the roof of a model house that looks suspiciously like the shop they are in.

"This is the only thing I repair by hand," the white-haired octogenarian says. "Every few hundred years I fix all the tearings and decay, and make it anew . . . to remember who I used to be."

He chances a look at the younger man. "I like your shoes," he says, and then he goes back to the roof, nudging his glasses to a higher point on his nose.

The one with the nice shoes glances down and softly curses. On his feet he's wearing neon green second-skin sport shoes that cling to him from the toes to the ankles. He says he had been so preoccupied with the travel ahead of him that he had forgotten to check if he was 'wearing age-appropriate footwear'.

The older one only guffaws in response.

The younger one smiles, and then straightens up. His

demeanour is serious now. "You talked about the 'balm of time', and when I asked you . . ."

The white-haired one interrupts him, and says, "The third time you ask me the question, we'll be at the hospital, next to Lifegiver. Rekha will be there, too. The questions you three will ask me, from your own distinct perspectives, will lead to the idea of my current form."

"I still don't understand," the younger man replies. He seems a bit agitated. "If you already know everything, why can't you just tell me?"

"That's not true, Samay. I don't know everything. I know how to operate . . . this gift. I don't know the mechanical aspect of it. *You* are the one who designs my inner workings—who draws up the schematics, who builds the prototypes, and tests its powers—based on the conversation all four of us will have at the hospital."

"So you can't give me the full picture . . ." the man with the green shoes starts.

"Because you haven't drawn it up yet," the old man responds.

"Another thing I don't understand," the younger man asks, "is why you couldn't just tell me all of this? Why did you make me travel all the way to three different years? What was the point of that?"

"Would you have believed me if I'd just told you these things? About the shop, about Jaya and Subhash, about me?"

"Of course, I would have," the younger man says with a bit of force.

"I might tell you all sorts of things and in principle you might believe them, but unless you live through an experience, unless you see things for yourself, you will never truly come to terms with reality. Which is why you had to see customers come in and out; you had to see the shop as a functioning entity. Everyone needs some form of proof."

"This reminds me—Rekha is not quite sure about . . . your transformation. She fears you will lose your memories, or suppress them. She's had a discussion with Dara, but still she is unsure," the green-shoed man says.

"It's a valid fear, but I assure you, Samay, I remember everything," says the old man as he takes his time to close the lid over the can of varnish and place it back on a shelf behind him.

"Wait," the other man says. "If you remember everything, if you . . . remember us, why didn't you ever come meet us?"

"If I'd met you, told you about what was about to happen, you'd have tried to save Lifegiver in 1950. Don't argue with me," he says, when the younger man opens his mouth. "It's human nature to want to change something that cannot be changed. But more importantly, do you remember the terms and conditions of time travel? The very first one?"

"I will not alter any important, far-reaching events." The sentence is delivered in a monotone.

"If, somehow, you were to save me, I wouldn't have the drug-addled dream, and plant the idea in your head. And then none of this would happen."

"But I could still . . ." the young one protests.

"No, Samay. Even if either of us had the same idea, the way we'd go about it would be different, the external factors that influenced our decisions now would be different. *I* would be different. Some things are just meant to be. You have to learn to accept things." Saying so, he looks at the younger man expectantly, waiting for something.

For a few seconds neither speaks, and then the old man opens the workshop door and gestures for the younger one to follow him. As they pass the threshold, the latter wonders why the white-haired man's Lifegiver never thought to visit the shop before his accident. "What stopped him from doing so?" the young man asks.

"He was afraid. As simple as that. He was afraid he'd look for the shop in this time and find it in ruins, or worse, erased from the Earth. There was a great fear in Lifegiver that stopped him from searching," the old man says as he switches off the lights and opens the door to the shop. "Close the main door on your way out, it has a self-locking mechanism in place." The green-shoed man follows the octogenarian out of the shop in a daze. He seems quite overwhelmed with the events and revelations of the past few hours, and he leaves the door ajar a bit. The old man, who is a few steps ahead of him, turns around and looks back at him. "What's wrong?"

"Was that all? Was there no other reason to send me back?" the young one asks.

The white-haired man's eyes start to glow. "Aah," he says. "I was wondering when you'd ask me this question. I was waiting . . ."

". . . for the right moment. I know."

The old man laughs delightedly. "Sorry, Samay. But we have to play by the rules. We have to follow the flow of time."

"Now, where was I?" he adds. "Oh yes. The customer at the

shop in 2016. Do you remember seeing her, Samay? She had a radio with her?"

"Yes, I do. It was only a few minutes ago."

"And do you remember the first case of time travel that caught public attention, that made people realise the world was changing?"

"Yes. I read about it in school . . . oh."

The old man nods his head knowingly. "When I met her, and saw the radio in her hands I instantly knew who she was. Her presence confirmed what I'd been wondering about for a long time." He pauses and takes a step closer. Now they are only six feet apart.

"You see," he continues, "I already knew what my repaired objects were capable of. But what I didn't know was that the more I sent out these *evolved* radios and projectors into the world, the more I made time itself more . . . mobile."

"So what you are saying is . . ." the younger man says, eyes wide. "All this while people have been searching for the source of time travel—they have travelled to far and wide periods in history—when it's always been you. You were the one who started it all?"

"Indeed, Samay."

"Weren't you scared? Not of what you were creating, but weren't you scared that your customers might find out and want to manipulate you, or harm you in some way?"

"That's where your memory chime comes in," the white-haired one responds. "Once I realised the risks to what I was doing, once I realised who Inaya truly was, I took inspiration from your lovely chime and applied its principles to everything

I repaired from thereon. The moment they'd try to operate on their own, for the first time, they'd instantly forget *where* they got the object repaired from. It's sort of like a permanent solar eclipse that blocks a certain part of your memory."

"That's an interesting analogy, Arun," the younger man says.

The white-haired man beams at him. "Do you know what my name means?"

The one with the green shoes shakes his head.

"It can mean many things in Sanskrit—dawn, or the reddish sky in the early morning. Or just . . . the sun. The omnipresent entity that keeps a watch over us, that spreads joy and warmth from the east to the west."

"And what about the dark side? What about night?"

"It's only at night when you can clearly look at the stars and planets above, and realise how small you are in the grand scheme of things. It's only then that you can understand your true worth," the older man easily replies.

"You're talking like a god."

"When you've lived as long as I have, seen both the good and bad in people—it makes you an expert of sorts on humanity."

The younger man still appears cautious. "Why do I feel like you're still hiding things from me?" he asks.

The white-haired man guffaws. "Because I am. I told you: there's a right moment for everything. Which reminds me, and this is very important—we can't share every single detail we've discussed here, today, with either Rekha or my Lifegiver. Or even the Freshborn. Everyone has to figure things out at their own pace. So just follow my lead when we meet them, okay?" he says.

"Wait a second," the man with the green shoes says. "What's a Freshborn?"

"Oh, that's just a medical slang. Freshborn is what the doctors call synthetics when they are newly hatched. It takes them weeks to acclimatise to their surroundings."

"Will the Freshborn be okay to go so far back in time? Won't he feel lost?"

"You forget who he is, Samay," the older one responds. "I am him. He is me. I have already lived his life, and I know everything will be fine."

"Okay. Okay. And where will you be all that time?" the young man says. "I know time moves differently for you. But you can't really disclose that to everyone else, can you? Then they'll know your secret."

"That's a good point," the white-haired man says, grinning. "If only I had a disguise . . . something that would . . . Oh wait," he adds, as he digs into the pocket of his kurta and takes out a crumpled tissue that unfolds into an oval shape. "I always keep one in my pocket, just in case. Do you know what it is?"

"It's a sheet mask," the young one responds as he watches the older one lay the tissue on his skin. The once-white hair transforms to a bright pink, the eyes get bigger (supported by a bushier set of eyebrows), the wrinkles flatten out and disappear, the lips get smaller, and the cheeks get dusty with a layer of three-day old pink stubble on it. The ears, for some reason, stay unchanged.

"So you'll wear a mask the entire time in public?" the young man asks. He seems a bit uncomfortable with the old man's now-youthful face.

"For a while, yes. Once the Freshborn is released from the hospital, we will work on his core processor and send him to the 1950s. And *I* will take over his place in 7100. Everyone here will think me to be him and everyone in the past will think the Freshborn to be my Lifegiver." The young-old man softens his gaze. "I'm sorry," he adds. "This must be very confusing to you."

"It is," comes the answer. "And it also brings up a few questions in my mind."

"Such as?"

"What you said before, about having a responsibility to help people . . ."

"All of that is true," the pink-haired one says. "That is most definitely the motivation behind all the time I spent in the past, fixing and repairing. But the reason why all this has to happen is because my life, and yours, is essentially . . ."

"A loop."

"Exactly," the young-old man says, and then looks beyond the other man as something catches his eye.

He extends his left arm, the shorter one, in front of him, and a click is sounded off. The entire arm then stretches in length—beyond the right arm, covering the distance between them, past the green-shoed man, and closes the main door. As it returns to its original position, on its way, the arm lands a hand on the other man and pats his shoulder, even as the man in question looks on in surprise.

"It's been a tough day for you, hasn't it?" the young-old one asks.

The one with the green shoes turns his head and looks at the extended hand on his shoulder still.

"Oh these?" the pink-haired man says. "I updated them in the 50th century, when I took complete control of the shop. It was a few decades after the Synthetic Rights Commission was established."

He lowers his hand and grabs hold of the other man's arm, gently dragging him forward. "Now come along. I don't remember us being late for this."

"Late for what? Where exactly are we going?"

"To the hospital," the young-old man replies. "Lifegiver will be waking up soon."

Story Timeline

1935 – Samay meets Arun/Dadaji and Rekha in Chandni Chowk

1949 – Samay presents the prototype of the repair shop to Arun

1950 – Arun gets injured when the Ghantaghar collapses

1986 – Maurice visits Arun's shop

1994 – Paritosh visits Arun's shop

2016 – Inaya visits Arun's shop

4016 – Orko 23 talks to Inaya on the radio for the first time

7085 – Samay breaks the vase and travels to 1935

7100 – Samay meets a changed Arun

Acknowledgements

I'd like to thank E.D.E. Bell, the force behind Atthis Arts, for her guidance and patience during the editing process. My thanks also goes out to Chris Bell, the other creative half of Atthis Arts.

I'd like to thank all those who read the novella and provided their inputs. From friends who read very early drafts to beta readers who read a version of the manuscript that was closer to the finished product—I would like to express my deep gratitude to Nikita Puri, Smita Chakravarty, Aastha Sharma, Zarah Ahmad, Gwynn Bell, M. Kaur, Jeremiah Harlin, Jennifer Lee Rossman, Kella Campbell, Minerva Cerridwen, Valerie Linebaugh, Sasha Kasoff Moore, and Eva Maderbacher for lending their time and effort to the project.

I would also like to thank Sheila Burke and her dog-son Charlie for being incredible hosts in Dublin, where I wrote the first draft of *One Arm Shorter Than The Other*.

Lastly, I'd like to thank my parents for their support. They read each and every draft—providing valuable feedback of their own—and also motivated me when I got stuck with bouts of writer's block.

Gigi Ganguly, September 2021

About the Author

Gigi Ganguly is a writer of speculative fiction, with a Masters in Creative Writing from the University of Limerick in Ireland. She shifts her residence from Delhi to the Himalayas, depending on the season. This is her first novella.

You can follow Gigi online at gigiganguly.wordpress.com.

Printed in Great Britain
by Amazon